# KENDRA STERLING

## Grace to Beat the Odds

*This book is dedicated to the God of Abraham, Issac, and Jacob. I am your humble servant. Thank you for your guidance and your calling. Even though I told you no twice. I am happy now that I obeyed you. I love you Abba.*

# Contents

# Chapter 1

ONE THING FOR SURE, TWO THINGS FOR
CERTAIN

We start this journey in the summer of 1989 on the south side of Chicago. Englewood to be exact. At a nightclub called Tastie. Heads turn as Christina Harvey and her girls walk in the door.

"Aaayeee! that's my song."

Christina says as they head to the dance floor. They were too cool for school baby. Christina had on her cropped red and black leather jacket. A black spandex body suit, with red, calf high, leather boots. She had a red Kente cloth hat with the sharpest bob haircut. If you ran your finger through it, you were definitely pulling back a nub.

She topped her outfit off with a gold rope chain, large gold hoop earrings, and some red glasses that were so big she could see from Lowe all the way to the Dan Ryan. If you know, you know. Christina was short some would say, thicka than a snicka, beautifully melanated with chestnut brown eyes. She was the baddest in the club. the DJ plays the next hit. *doo... doo...da...doo...doo...follow me...follow meeeeeee*. The whole club made their way to the dance floor. One thing about Chicago, we don't play about our house music. We gone dance baby.

While Christina was dancing, a man comes up behind her. Dark chocolate, tall, and muscular sporting a high-top fade with a thick, black, and freshly lined up chin strap. He had on a red and white track suit with the shirt open. Two long gold chains laid perfectly against his chiseled chest. On his feet, he was rocking some red, black, and white kicks. Christina looked back at him. *Damn he fine.* She smiled and they danced together for the rest of the song. Afterwards, he walked with her to the bar.

"Can I buy you a drink?"

Christina smiles and gives him an affirming nod.

"I'm Mike!"

"Christina!"

They exchanged numbers and the rest was history. Mike made sure Christina was well taken care of. They would hit all the popular spots in da city. Yes I said *da city*. Argue with ya mama not me. Mike even bought a house in Bronzeville to be closer to her. After about 2 months of dating, he asked her to quit her job and move in with him. Mike told her,

"All I want you to do is stay fly and wait for me to get home."

Before he slid her some money. *I finally met my Prince.* Christina had the biggest smile on her face. You see, Mike was a truck driver not only was he a truck driver he also owned his own trucking company. So, Mike would be on the road weeks at a time. When Mike wasn't on the road he spent as much time with Christina as possible. He never wanted Christina out of his sight.

1990, New Year's Day. Christina got a phone call from Mike. *Hey baby, I need you to get dressed up. I'm coming to pick you up.* Shortly after, a sleek black limo pulled up in front of the house. Christina didn't know what to do. *Aw naw somebody died, he's taking me to a funeral.* Whole time, for some people if they saw a limo in Englewood, you automatically thought somebody died. Her heart started to beat out of her chest. *Well, let me get dressed.*

Christina stepped outside wearing a stunning black velvet, A-symmetrical long sleeved, split-thigh dress. Elegant black stilettos, Diamond earrings, Matching necklace, and a black clutch purse. Her hair was in a curled up-do with a swoop to the side. Her hair was every bit of fried, dyed, and laid to the side. Mike was star struck as he gazed at Christina with a bouquet of roses in his hand. She chuckled,
"You might want to close your mouth, before a fly get in there."

She gave him a kiss, thanked him for the flowers, and got in like she was born to ride in a limo.

"Ok who died?"

Mike looked at her with a mix of confusion and amusement.
"What are you talking about? We goin on a date. not to a
funeral. I gotta get you outta Englewood dang."

They pulled up to one of the hottest restaurants in town. Christina was excited because she heard their food was fye. Mike and Christina tore that food up. It wasn't a crumb left on them plates. Mike ordered a bottle of their best champagne and sprinkled some rose petals on the table, While Christina was in the bathroom. By the time Christina came back to the table Mike was already down on one knee holding a small box. Nestled in the black velvet ring box was a gorgeous oval 3 stone 14-karat diamond ring. Christina stood stunned. Tears started to fall down her face.

"Christina, I have loved you since I laid eyes on you. I knew then that I wanted you to be my wife. Christina, will you marry me?"

Mike held his breath, as he waited for her reply.

"Yes!"

Christina exclaimed as she gave him her left hand. Everyone cheered while Mike put the ring on her finger. This was the happiest day of Christina's life. The man of her dreams just asked for her hand in marriage.

About three months after their wedding, Christina started to feel nauseous when she woke up in the morning. She paid it no mind. She even thought that her weight gain was just happy weight. She wasn't surprised when her menstrual cycle didn't come, she had issues with her menstrual cycle in the past. When it was time for Christina to go for her routine checkup. The Doctor gave her a pregnancy test. The test came back positive, Christina was so excited. She couldn't wait to tell Mike. She started to plan how she would tell him when he got home from taking a load to New York. *This has to be special.* Christina cooked all of Mike's favorite food. Steak, loaded baked potato, broccoli with cheese, and apple pie topped with vanilla ice cream for dessert. She lit candles to set the ambiance for the big reveal. She bought a pink *I'm a Girl Dad* shirt, a pacifier, and a bottle to go with the sonogram picture of their little bundle. She wrapped up the gift in a beautiful pink gift bag with pink tissue paper covering.

Christina couldn't wait for Mike to walk through the door.

# Chapter 1

When he did, Mike had the biggest smile on his face looking at the beautiful spread Christina laid out.

"Dang Baby you really missed me huh?"

He gave her a kiss, washed his hands, and proceeded to bust that food down. When he was finished, Mike smiled and rubbed his stomach.

"That food was fye Queen."

In her sweetest voice, Christina replied,

"I'm glad you liked it king, I got a surprise for you."

Christina placed the gift bag in front of him. Mike looked confused at the color of the bag as he opened it. Mike looked in the bag and his confused look turned into scorn. He slowly looked at Christina.

"I thought you was on birth control?"

"I was, but with the wedding and everything I forgot one of my doses."

He stood up, looked Christina in the eye for a moment.

"You knew I didn't want no kids."

He stood calmly. His swing was so fast Christina almost didn't see him back hand her. She fell to the ground. Mike began to punch her body strategically avoiding her face. She was able to kick him off, giving her just enough time to run out the front door. Mike ran after her. He caught up with her just as she made it to the front porch. Wasting no time, He pushed her down the front steps. Mike stood over her briefly before he stormed off to his car and pulled off.

Christina slowly sat up from the fetal position she was lying in; she felt something wet between her legs.

"Is that blood?"

# Chapter 2

## IS THIS LOVE?

The doctors determined that the placenta had detached itself and Christina needed an emergency c-section. They rushed her to surgery. The surgery was touch and go.

July 25th, 1990 was the day I, Olivia Bailey, opened my eyes for the first time. I remember being told later that my mama didn't even want to look at me. They said it was something called post partum depression and that it was rather common for mothers to go through it.

I was in the N.I.C.U for almost two months due to being born prematurely. It was a rocky road, I almost died multiple times. The doctors said that it was a miracle I survived. Mama came around eventually she would visit me while I was in the incubator. She never came close. She would just watch from a distance then leave. Mama and Daddy got divorced. Not to much of a surprise there. Mama didn't want to press charges on him for hurting her though.

I found out later that Uncle Brandon made a phone call and my daddy decided to never put his hands on another woman again. Daddy even came to visit me. He started to claim me after the D.N.A test. He tried apologizing to Mama, she almost got back with him until granny Odessa told her,

"If a man hits you once, he is sure to hit you again. And you might not survive the second hit."

Mama agreed with granny Odessa. That was the end of that relationship. Me and Mama were never really close. I felt like she blamed me for her and daddy not being together. One time she told me,

"I should've aborted you."

I guess we both had wounds to heal.

We were at everybody's house but ours most days. The healing journey was rocky. Mama chose to distract herself with friends and drinking. I wasn't mad that she chose that avenue. All I wanted was for her to be happy. Unfortunately, most of the time my happiness was a distant thought to her.

One night we had a sleepover at one of her friend's house, I didn't want to stay but something about mama's slurred speech told me driving home wasn't such a good idea. I was only 7, but I could tell that she had been drinking. I remember lying in the bed surrounded by kids I didn't know visualizing my grandparents walking through the door and rescuing me. I could almost hear the sound of door opening, then someone kicked me, and I snapped back to reality. I cried myself to sleep that night.

My grandparents did eventually catch wind of what was

going on. They decided to take custody of me. I was happy they did. Mama needed more time to heal. I was especially happy to be around my Pawpaw Ezekiel. Me and Pawpaw always had a special bond. I was told that even as a baby I only wanted to be held by him. Pawpaw was honorably discharged from the Marines after the Vietnam war. Me and Pawpaw would go everywhere together, there was rarely a time that you saw him and not me.

Pawpaw loved teaching life lessons. Lectures to be more specific. There were times when Pawpaw would lecture me for literally hours about life. I would fall asleep on him, wake up, and he would still be talking. When I complained about him being long winded he would say,
"Olivia, it's a situation to wheres, one day you'll actually want to hear me teach you these things and I won't be here to teach you"
I just sat back in the most melodramatic way possible and rolled my eyes, thinking the lecture would never end. Which did nothing but make him chuckle before he continued his lecture.

Daddy would come to pick me up sometimes. I always enjoyed our time together. One day he came to pick me up to take me to the movies. We had so much fun I didn't want the day to end.
"Ok did you have fun?".
Daddy asked as we left.
"Yes!"
I exclaimed. He then informed me that I was going to stay the night with him. When I got to his house, I took a bath while daddy popped popcorn. We got our blankets and made a spot on the couch. When the movie ended, I felt a tap on my

shoulder.

"Come here baby and give Daddy a hug."

When I hugged him, he picked me up. He rocked me slowly and rubbed my back.

"You know Daddy loves you so much, right?"

"Yes Daddy, I love you too" I replied.

I felt so loved. Then Daddy took me by the hand, and led me to his bedroom.

He showed me he loved me a lot after that.

# Chapter 3

## WORK IN PROGRESS…

I was so confused about what love was. I just knew what my dad was doing didn't feel right. I didn't fully understand the feelings I was having. There was a new sensation in a place I had never felt before.

I felt dirty. I felt used and tainted. I had so many emotions flowing through me, and I didn't know what to do with them. I couldn't talk to anyone about it because, dad made me promise not to tell anyone. I was forced to endure this alone, plagued by confusion for two years.

I would go over my dad's mom, grandma Shirley, house on the weekends with my little brother and my cousins on my daddy side, we would play this game called 'House'.

In the game of 'House' everybody would partner up as 'Mommy and Daddy'. One person would pretend to be the child. You would go to a separate area of the playroom and play like you raising a family for a split second. Then when you put the play kids to sleep, the 'mommy and daddy' would go 'freak'.

We would usually wait until grandma fell asleep. Then we would go down in the basement and play 'House'. After a while, when her nap was over, grandma would check on us and we would act like nothing was happening. Grandma Shirley was strict and very wise, but we were some sneaky kids. We never got caught.

After a while all of this 'Love' started to overwhelm me. One day Pawpaw saw me crying in the back seat after he picked me up from my dad's house. We were on our way home when he asked me.

"what's wrong baby girl?"

I looked down and told him nothing was wrong. He then asked me,

"Then why are you crying?"

I looked out the window, took a deep breath and said,

"My Daddy shows me that he loves me every time I go to his house and now, I'm confused about what love is Pawpaw."

Pawpaw got quiet for a second, then he asked me,

"What do you mean by he shows you that he loves you?"

I then described to him exactly what my daddy's definition of 'Love' meant. Pawpaw didn't say anything else during the rest of the ride, but when I looked out the window he was speeding to the house.

When we got home Pawpaw finally spoke and told Granny Odessa to call my mama.

Pawpaw gestured for me to come to him, he held me tight and said,

"Ok baby girl, tell them what happened."

I did as I was instructed, when I was done my mama yelled out curse words I had never heard before and stormed out of the house. My granny started sobbing and Pawpaw just held me tighter.

When Granny stopped crying, she called the police. Pawpaw told me everything was going to be alright. They took me to the hospital to do a rape kit, I screamed and took off running. They had to strap me to the bed.

By the time we were on our way back to the house, they had arrested my father. It was so weird being 10 years old with a lawyer.

I experienced so many emotions during the case. I had to describe what happened repeatedly. They gave me a doll to point to the body parts he defiled. Even though this process was necessary to the case, I found myself just constantly reliving it in my head. Not to mention coming to the realization that what I thought was 'love' was actually me being mentally and emotionally manipulated to accept, enjoy, and help cover up being abused.

I felt dirty, like I could never be clean again. I felt so stupid, how could I allow myself to believe, that was love. Anger began to creep in.

"I TRUSTED HIM!"

"HE WAS SUPPOSED TO KEEP ME SAFE!"

"HE WAS SUPPOSED TO BE MY PROTECTOR NOT MY ABUSER!"

I didn't know who to trust anymore, I was numb to all relationships. I was more confused than ever before. I still loved my father and wanted no harm to come to him.

My father was sentenced to 2 years in jail, 2 years on parole, he was not allowed to see me until I turned 18, and he had to register as a sex offender for the rest of his life. I had to do court ordered therapy until the age of 15. It was time to pick up the pieces of my life and try to put them back together again.

At my first therapy session I was so angry. I spent most of the session screaming and crying. I had an amazing therapist named Mrs. Gardner; she allowed me to vent as I pleased for at least the first 5 sessions until I got it all out. After that, then we started to deconstruct each of my feelings one by one. I was not ready for the deconstruction; I wanted to stay angry and live there forever.

We started with understanding how my dad's brain operated. I expressed that this was going to be rough for me, but Mrs. Gardner assured me that she would help me every step of the way. She helped me to understand that my dad had a mental illness. It took me a little longer to conclude that the abuse didn't happen because I was bad, ugly, or stupid.

The mental illness was a result of my father not taking the time to heal from the abuse that he endured. I learned that when it comes to trauma, what isn't transformed is transferred. We talked about the flashbacks I was experiencing. We talked about the night terrors I was having every night that would have me waking up screaming, in a cold sweat, and not knowing where I was.

One night Pawpaw was making his usual rounds around the house at night. When he came to check on me, he saw my leg out from under the covers. He had no idea that I was in the middle of a nightmare where the grim reaper was sitting right where pawpaw was standing. The grim reaper reached his hand out to grab my ankle at the exact time pawpaw was trying to put my leg back under the cover. I jumped up, screamed, and scared both of us.

We laughed about it later but boy, oh boy it was not funny in that moment. Pawpaw had become used to my night terrors eventually. I later learned that Pawpaw had night terrors too, especially after the war. The main reason he did his rounds at night was because of his night terrors.

Every night that I woke up screaming, Pawpaw was right there. He would tuck me back in then sit with me and we would talk about life until I went back to sleep. Some nights I would just lay my head on his chest and just listen to his heartbeat until I fell asleep.

I talked to my therapist about how Pawpaw helped me, and she explained to me that my relationship with my grandfather is how a father and daughter relationship was supposed to be. I felt blessed to finally have an example of a father through my grandfather. Although I was in a lot of emotional pain, I knew that this was a part of God's grace.

I even learned to enjoy Pawpaw's long-winded talks. My favorite thing to talk to him about was his war stories. He would tell me about how he survived three ambushes in Vietnam. Somethings he would never speak about. I didn't understand why but, I never pushed the issue.

Me and pawpaw were big movie lovers. To the point where we would fuss all the time about who had who's movie. Somehow, he always thought I had his movie.

Our bond was so beautiful. Having moments like this really helped me with my P.T.S.D. I started to feel my fight or flight mode flare up less and less.

For a while I felt as if men only wanted to get close to me to hurt me. Pawpaw showed me something completely different. I still had a long way to go though.

I got suspended like clockwork for fighting bullies, all of them being boys. I was never one to start a fight, but if you bullied me, or anyone I was cool with, I was ready to go 12 rounds with you. I remember fighting one bully three times because he messed with me once. The first two times I lost the fight, so I kept fighting with him until I got him that third time.

I understood that I wouldn't win every fight, but I would fight every day until I did. I would go from 0 to 100, I never had a middle ground. When I was in fight or flight mode I chose to fight over flight.

Despite all the fights I had, school was really my outlet. Surprisingly my grades soared during this time. I would let my schoolwork be my escape from the trials in my life. I loved learning, it really helped me not feel so stupid anymore. I was starting to feel like I was really stepping into a breakthrough.

It was a long hard road. But, God has had me covered since before I was born. So, I knew that He would continue to guide me through the tribulations.

My Granny Odessa kept me in church every Sunday. Shoot sometimes I was at church more than I was at home. Mondays was usher board meeting, Tuesdays was bible study, Thursdays was choir rehearsal, and Saturdays was nursing board meeting. Not to mention Sunday school before the sermon.

We would have Sunday dinner at church, and then, what felt like, a 4-hour long afternoon service. Oh, and don't let us go visit another church. Sometimes we wouldn't get out of church until almost midnight. Although our dedication to church was a full-time job, I loved every minute of it. I found God and developed a relationship with Him. That relationship was the biggest blessing I could ever ask for. The blessing of a parent's agape love.

One night me and my grandparents were having dinner. We sat down and just when we started to eat, we heard the doorbell ring. My Mama walks into the dining room and announces that she is moving to another state with her new boyfriend. She told me she loved me, kissed me on the forehead, and proceeded to walk out the front door. I sat there with the fork in my hand, completely stunned. Pawpaw just sat there and looked at me.

I couldn't find the words to say, as the tears began to fall, my eyes finally found Pawpaw's eyes. In that moment I knew I had more things to work on with my therapist.

My healing was a work in Progress...

*Chapter 4*

## THEY WERE JUST CHILDREN

Me and my therapist Mrs. Gardner started to zone in on me and my mother's relationship. I explained to her my feelings that I had about her and we started our deconstruction process. Mrs. Gardner helped me to understand that my Mama was behaving like a person who hasn't healed from her past trauma.

We discussed the dynamics of mama's other relationships and how the negative impact of those relationships affected how my mama handled situations concerning me. We continued to navigate what that meant and how to heal from it. Mrs. Gardner explained that my mother was still internally hurt by her past. She told me that mama chose flight in her fight or flight mode. In one of our meetings we talked about how her choice to flee was really a choice not to face what was really hurting her. Mrs. Gardner taught me that to truly heal from what trauma we have to face the trauma.

We worked on healing until my last appointment right before I entered my freshman year in high school. I had many breakthroughs during our sessions. We worked on my trust issues, forgiving my parents, my abandonment issues, my genuine distaste for men, and a host of other issues.

"Well, Olivia I hope that I was able to help you."

Mrs. Gardner said in our last session. I still struggled with some things, but the court appointed sessions were over. The last 5 years were rocky, but God had His hand on me.

A lot of changes started to happen for me back-to-back. During the time my mom was away, she gave birth to my stepsister Diamond. They eventually moved back to Illinois. Me and my grandparents moved to the south suburbs, after mugs kept shooting in the alley behind our house.

I realized that I was becoming interested in women. I didn't want to wear female clothes anymore because it brought attention from men. The femininity that I didn't want for myself, was something I found attractive in women. My flesh and my spirit were at war. I was becoming overwhelmed with the transitions in my life.

One day me and my grandparents went to one of Pawpaw's routine doctor visits. Dr. Rick examined him and determined that he had Alzheimer's. We didn't fully understand the gravity of the diagnosis. When we got the news, Pawpaw was still in his right mind to us.

I switched my focus to preparing for freshman year. I was very nervous about starting this new journey in life. The freshman pep rally got us all hyped to conquer the world that helped with my nerves. I couldn't wait to get home and tell my grandparents.

When I explained what happened on my first day to Pawpaw, I noticed that it confused him. That was when it really set in that Pawpaw had Alzheimer's. I hugged him and I held my tears until I got to my room. Reality hit me like an 18-wheeler to the stomach.

My Pawpaw.

My Hero.

My Protector.

He was forgetting more and more. I was confused and angry. He didn't deserve this. He was the greatest man I ever knew. *Why did he have to go through this?* His symptoms were accelerating. He was declining more and more every day. This was all happening so fast for me. Too fast. *They said it would be a LONG goodbye!*

This didn't seem very long to me. I felt myself starting to panic. The anxiety started to set in. *Will He forget me? How would I survive without my him!?*

I took some deep breaths. Although Pawpaw was becoming more forgetful and confused, he was not dead. I refused to mourn him like he was. Internally I felt broken, but externally I had to be strong for my soldier. Anytime I cried growing up Pawpaw would always say,

"Stop crying baby girl. It's going to be ok. Wash your face."

I planned to do just that.

I redirected my energy to my freshman year in high school. They announced auditions for the speech team during morning announcements. I was ready to dive into everything high school had to offer. I could really use a distraction from my home life.

I auditioned and made the team. I was placed in the Prose category. I had never paid much attention to poetry. As I researched a piece to compete with, I found out that I really enjoyed reading it. The melody of each expression spoke to my soul. It felt as if I was born to read it.

I was introduced to my coach Ms. Dell. She was a very passionate actress, dancer, and coach. I loved how she knew exactly how to motivate and inspire me during each practice. I learned that if Ms. Dell throws something at you and hits you with a *YAAAASSSS!* Then you know you did something right. She always knew how to see greatness in us.

Our tournaments were held on Saturdays. We would wake up with Jesus at 4am and be on the bus at school by 5am. Our uniform was all black, business casual, with a splash of color. When we got to our designated classroom, we got our room assignments. After that it was time to get a brief practice before heading to compete. When I walked into my assigned room, I took my seat and waited my turn to perform in front of the class.

I started to feel a little nervous, but I quickly prayed the nerves away. When it was my turn to perform my piece, I took a deep breath and gave it all I had. My first tournament turned out to be amazing and I won first place in my category.

After that, the season felt like a blur. I didn't make it to Regionals in my individual category, but I still had an opportunity.

I chose to audition for the Performance in the Round (P.I.R) category that would compete in Regionals with the individual categories. The P.I.R was a shortened play performed by a small group of individuals. The play had to take place in a circle that had been taped out on the ground with four openings that would serve as the entrance/exits. The group had to perform in the circle, they could not step outside of the circle during the performance. If they even stepped on the line, it would be an immediate disqualification. So, the stakes were high.

I auditioned at the P.I.R auditions and I made the team. I was super excited on our first day of rehearsal. We had three coaches for this P.I.R, Ms. Dell, Mr. Peters, and Mr. Harvey.

Our coaches wrote an original script called *"They Were Children"*. The script was about the real-life church bombing that killed four little girls. We loved the script and were excited about telling the four little girls' story.

We realized the gravity of it. We took our roles seriously and left our hearts in that circle every practice. We practiced before and after school. We knew that script like the back of our hand.

When it was our turn to perform at Regionals, we told their stories with everything in us. We didn't think about winning, we wanted people to know that their lives mattered. We wanted them to feel the depth of the tragedy that happened to them. When we were done, many people in the room, including the judges, had tears rolling down their faces. A lot of people had no idea that the bombing had ever happened. This script was literally changing people's lives right in front of us.

The awards ceremony included the individual categories and the P.I.R category. After the individual events were called, they began to call the P.I.R category. We won first place in the Regionals P.I.R category. This was no longer just a competition; this was bigger than us. This was even bigger than winning.

We really got hyped after that. We refocused and practiced even harder. Sectionals were next and we would be competing against more schools. For us it was just more people to educate.

We won first place in Sectionals. We didn't even know it was possible to take it up a notch in practice, but we did. State finals were next, so the pressure was on. We had to beat over 200 other schools in the P.I.R category alone. We were one of three all black teams competing, and our script was about a murder that happened because of racism. I think pressure was an understatement.

Our coaches requested we have a separate room from the individual events. The moment we walked past the threshold of that classroom we were in character. We were locked in; we didn't even leave the room until it was time to do our final run-through.

"This is it ladies, I only want you to tell their stories. Focus. Don't worry about the competition or the judges. Leave it all in the circle."

Ms. Dell said before we prayed and headed to the circle. Everything boiled down to this moment.

As we walked into the P.I.R room in our all-white attire, the room was packed. All chairs were taken, and people were literally standing on the walls. It was so quiet in the room. We walked to our entry points. Ms. Dell hit play on the boom box. We walked into the circle and proceeded to tell those girl's stories as if our lives depended on it. When we exited the circle, no one could stop the tears from flowing down their faces.

Later as we all walked back to our classroom. The minute the door closed behind us, our head coach Mrs. Pace looked at us and said,

"I need to tell you something."

Then she paused. The suspense was too much, I wanted to yell out *WHAT WOMAN!*

# Chapter 4

"You just won the state championship."

She said in a calm tone. It took us a second to register it because she said it so calmly. Then, we all started screaming joyfully. We hugged each other, then our screams turned into loud sobbing. Not because we won, it was far beyond us. No, we were sobbing for those 4 little girls that were murdered. Who had their whole lives ahead of them. Who did nothing to the men who decided to attack that church, taking their lives. Who never got to see their 16th birthday. We mourned for them. They didn't deserve that.

*THEY WERE JUST CHILDREN.*

# Chapter 5

## THE PATH LEAST TRAVELED

The final event of the speech season was Group Interpretation (GI). GI is kind of like P.I.R, but instead of a smaller circle you have a larger square.

Our head coach Mrs. Pace chose a short story from 1969 to be our GI piece. This short story was based off real-life events during the great depression. We read the short story and loved it. I was excited to work with our head coach Mrs. Pace.

Although we were never close, when we won state, she was so happy for us. The way she boasted about us and spoke of us with pride made me feel she really believed in us.

One time after a dress rehearsal, she had us bring her our uniforms and she ironed them. Afterwards she held a meeting with the whole team.

She said to us,

"you guys need to have better hygiene; I ironed your clothes and the smell that came off of them was horrible."

All while she was saying this statement, she was looking right at me. She might as well have said,

"I'm talking about you Olivia."

Some of my teammates started to look at me. Some even giggled. I felt so embarrassed. I hated the fact that she chose a public humiliation technique rather than private mentorship. I felt like the runt of the group. The one no one wanted there. I started to resent her for that. I noticed that Mrs. Pace didn't treat everyone like that. I guess I wasn't a part of her favorites group.

Mrs. Pace treated her favorites like royalty, she treated everyone else like a pheasant outcast. Through the drama, I stayed focused on the GI. I loved the story, so I put the distractions aside and put my all into rehearsals. We practiced hard and won first place in the regional tournament.

During practice breaks I found myself alone a lot. I tried to fit in but, I was still treated like the outcast. My attempts to fit in was met with,

"Ugh we Can't have nothing without somebody trying to be like us."

Apart of me wanted to bring out the old me and fight all of them, but I didn't want to get kicked off the speech team. I truly hated bullying and there were times when I felt surrounded by bullies. The only time I felt like I was a part of the team was during performances and when we heard our name called for a win. We would jump and cheer, everyone would hug each other. I would hold on to those moments. They were fleeting.

When we won second place at the state championship, I was

happier for the experience to be over than I was for winning 2nd place. I put my headphones on for the ride back to school. I was learning something about myself.  I didn't care about winning.

By the beginning of my junior year, my grade point average had suffered. Mrs. Pace wasted no time cutting me from the team because of it. I made the speech team my priority.  My grades reflected my focus or lack thereof. I felt overwhelmed. It felt like I was running up hill with chains and weights on me.

One day during free period I got my notebook and began to write,

"Phoenix

I was down for a moment

That's a fact

True blue

But the bounce back is crazy

Who is that?

A new you

This gift

God gave

My soul

God saved

Knocking out Goliath

They call me the new Dave"

How they treated me hurt but I couldn't allow myself to stay there. I had to regain my focus.

So, I buckled down and concentrated on my schoolwork. When I felt myself become overwhelmed I expressed myself through poetry. I felt like I was remembering my first passion. I was so consumed with the speech team that I was loosing sight of everything else I loved. *Me.*

At home, Pawpaw was declining faster than ever. He stopped wanting to take his meds. He barely wanted to eat. I gave him his meds and a snack when I got home from school every day. Somedays, he would fuss with me about eating, but I knew what he liked. I would make his favorite foods then I would hide his medicine in his food and feed it to him.

We started to notice that he was becoming more and more irritable. Things that didn't usually upset him would make him mad. Especially if he saw his car or bike.

Pawpaw loved to drive his car and ride his bike. Unfortunately, after his diagnosis, he started to get lost a lot. One time Pawpaw was lost for hours and when we called to see where he was, he couldn't tell us. It got so bad that granny had to sell his bike and car. The hardest part about this was knowing that I couldn't fix it for him.

Growing up it felt like Pawpaw had all the answers to every problem. It felt like it was nothing he couldn't solve. Watching his decline had become the hardest thing I ever had to watch. All I wanted to do was fix it for him like he fixed things for me growing up, but there was no fixing this.

I felt like I couldn't catch a break anywhere, I wanted to get back into therapy but, when I asked granny, she would say yes but never scheduled it. I knew granny had a lot on her plate, so I didn't push the issue. I felt like I needed someone to talk to, I tried talking to my other grandma. The conversations started off ok until she found out about my lifestyle. After that our conversations changed.

I felt like the only escape I had was my poetry. I did, however, meet this girl on a dating website. Her name was Michelle. I was grateful to have her in my life. We started talking then eventually we met up. We enjoyed every minute we spent together. After a couple of dates, We made our relationship official. Neither one of us had told anyone that we were lesbians. If anyone asked we just told them we were friends. We kept this lie going for a while.

One day we got caught kissing when granny came to pick me up from the restaurant, she had dropped me off at. She bout had a fit when she saw us. I let her know I have been in a relationship with a woman for a while. I informed her that I didn't know how to tell her. With everything going on I didn't want to overload her.

She stood stunned for a minute, then she punched me in my jaw. The punch was so unexpected that I fell backwards. The other punches hurt my soul more than they hurt me. After she was done, she performed an attempted exorcism. She called me an abomination and pleaded the blood of Jesus while she continued to punch me with both fists. *It feels like she hates me, this can't be Jesus.* She then kicked me out and said,

"You're an abomination, get out of my house and you bet not take nothing I bought with you either."

So, I left my grandparents' house sobbing with nothing but the pjs on my back and the cell phone I snuck out in my pocket. My mama came to pick me up, I ended up staying at her place for a few weeks. I felt completely broken, hurt, and betrayed. I thought my granny loved me more than that.

She attacked me like I was a demon from hell. I only loved a woman I wasn't hurting anybody. I became very depressed. I didn't want to eat or do anything. One day it became too much for me and I went into the kitchen and got a knife. Just as I was about to slice my wrist, my mama came into the kitchen and yelled,

"What the hell are you doing?!"

My depression seemed to be too much for my mama to handle so she sent me back to my grandparents' house. I felt like a washed-up rag doll that no one wanted. I was just being thrown back and forth. I was hoping to have a bonding moment with my mama but then I remembered that we have never been close. I don't know what made me think that would change when I was going through something.

When we got to the house, Pawpaw was at the door waiting as he always was. I hugged him so tight I couldn't stop the tears from falling. I really needed to talk to my hero. He was the one I went to in times like this. He always had some wisdom for moments like this.

I wanted things to be how they used to be so bad. Pawpaw was always the mediator of our family. He was the voice of reason. Pawpaw never let our disagreements go too far. He would always say,

"Alright now Odessa, that's enough."

or

"Olivia listen to your grandmother."

The memories made the tears flow faster. My Pawpaw would've never let me get kicked out.

When I made it into my room, I engulfed myself in my poetry.

"<u>Just let me be me</u>

Your words wrapped around my neck like an asphyxiating

string

Your hatred pulled tighter and tighter

Is this what love means?

Breathe in

Breathe out

You never know when it will be your last

D.O.A
Killed by the expectations that crashed
The pedestals never last
The knife in my back was a lesson
When I think about it
revealing your true colors was a blessing
Now I see you
Mask turned to cellophane
No peek-a-boo
I see the truth
Keep your bondage I prefer to be free
I will not assimilate
Just let me be me"

The next day at school I signed up for our school poetry slam. It was created by our librarian Mrs. Buckley. The library was packed. Our snaps was the ultimate ovation. Our silence was equivalent to a boo.

It became my second home. I remember Mrs. Buckley letting us know that the makeshift stage was a safe space. She gave everyone creative freedom to fully express themselves. She only had two rules, no cursing and no booing. I remember reciting 'Just Let Me Be Me'. I let out everything that I was feeling. It must have been a lot because when I was done, Mrs. Buckley gestured for me to take a deep breath.

I looked out at the audience; they sat stunned for a second then everybody started to snap. I started to think maybe this wasn't just a way of escape. Maybe I was meant to do this.

I didn't think about the speech team much after that. The poetry slams became my outlet. Right on time too because when my granny kicked me out again, she also went to my girlfriend's house and told her mama about our relationship.

I had confided in my uncle Brandon a while back when I asked him for a ride to Michelle's house. I expressed to him how I felt about women. He was the first person I talked to about it and he didn't judge me. I thought this moment had solidified our bond.

When Michelle called me telling me that my grandma had just left her house, I knew he took her, he was the only one who knew where she lived. I felt betrayed, that was the first time I realized I couldn't trust my uncle Brandon. I never trusted him again after that.

When my granny told her mom about us, Michelle's mom grounded her for lying. Her mom didn't care about her being gay. She just didn't like the fact that some random person told her something about her child that her child didn't tell her. I didn't hear from her for a long time.

I felt like my life was in a constant state of turmoil, but the saddest part was that I was starting to get used to it. These traumatic events started to feel like just another day for me. I started to accept that this was just life.

My best friend Tony was a blessing from God. We met freshman year and we didn't find out that we lived 2 blocks from each other until my junior year. When we found that out his house became a second home. His family accepted me as one of their own. I remember many nights kicking it in his backyard until late in the night. He really had my back during my rough times. He always had the best advice. He never judged me either.

My other best friend Brenda and I mostly hung out at school. We didn't get into the deeper issues of life, but we would turn any situation into nothing but laughter. God truly blessed me with good people in my circle in high school. Maybe the good was starting to outweigh the bad.

# Chapter 6

## YOU THOUGHT YOU BROKE ME?

I know it was nothing but the grace of God that I was able to get all my college applications out. It felt like God still sent His angels and the Holy spirit to cover me and rest on me, regardless of my sins. I even got a good score on my A.C.T. I never claimed to be perfect, but I knew when I got baptized at the age of 9 that me and God had a special bond. He was clearly showing me that my sins may have put a wedge between us, but it never changed the fact that He loved me.

I went into my senior year in a better mood about life. Clad with my Letterman's jacket and my class ring, I felt unstoppable.

I continued to pour my heart out at the poetry slams. It felt revolutionary. We gave messages of standing up for what was right. We talked of unity, resisting oppression, having good morals, and to never allow someone to piss on you and tell you it's raining. When we finished, we walked around the halls feeling like we could conquer the world.

I was in the middle of English class when Michelle texted me and said she was off punishment. My heart did 5 leaps. I was so happy I could do a back flip. I probably would've broken my neck, but I would've tried.

Although it felt good to talk to her she seemed distant. I know she had been on punishment for half of our junior year, but we never broke up or anything. Even in our stolen moments where she would email me, or I her, she always seemed to miss me as much as I missed her. So, I asked her,
"Dang baby why you being so distant?"
She paused for a while, then She took a deep breath, and said,
"I'm being distant because I got something that I have to tell you."
My stomach started to feel sick. *What's this about.* I thought we would just pick back up where we left off. I thought our love was strong enough to stand the test of time. I calmed myself down from my mini panic attack. Michelle continued,
"I have been thinking about what happened before I was grounded."
I held my breath. My mind was racing.*Where was this going? Why is she talking to me like she doesn't love me? She was my first love. I thought our bond was locked in for life.* I started to panic again as she continued to say,
"I saw how much I really hurt my mom by lying to her. That's when it hit me. I was too afraid that my mom would judge me like your grandma judged you. I allowed your life to influence me to lie to my mom. I realized that you are a bad influence

on my life. I would've never lied if it wasn't for you. I don't want to be in a relationship with someone who is a bad influence. It's over."

I laid in my bed staring at the ceiling with the phone still to my face even after she hung up. No matter how much I tried I couldn't close my mouth. Processing what she just said was out of the question. I couldn't do anything but lay there. Then a wail came out of me that I had never heard before. Thank God my grandma was at work. Pawpaw slowly made his way to the door of my room. He walked in to see me in the fetal position bawling my eyes out. He sat on the side of my bed and asked,

"What happened?"

Through my sobs I told him. He made me sit up. I laid my head on his shoulder as he said,

"Stop crying, you can't force people to do right by you. So hold your head up and remember who you are. Now go wash your face."

Pawpaw always knew how to speak life back into me. for a moment my Pawpaw was talking like his old self. *I think I just witnessed one of the lucid moments the doctor was talking about.*

Dr. Rickles explained that Pawpaw might have moments when he appeared as if he doesn't have Alzheimer's. Sometimes it can last a few hours, it could last a few minutes, and sometimes it would last only a few seconds. All I know is I thank God for that lucid moment. I truly needed it. I got myself together and washed my face. I refused to let this break me. Pawpaw was right, I needed to remember who I was.

Ezekiel's Granddaughter.

# Chapter 7

## NO WHERE TO GO BUT UP

Over the next couple of weeks, I started to get response letters from the colleges I applied to. I got a couple of denial letters. Waiting on my acceptance letters was the equivalent of waiting to see if I was getting inducted into the cool kid's club or going to the gauntlet. So much depended on it. The way my granny Odessa put it, if you didn't have a degree or a good job you were nothing. I really needed this acceptance letter.

Two weeks later after so many rejection letters came in the mail, I started to feel really doubtful and hopeless. Then it happened I got that letter that changed everything. Granny said,

"A letter came for you today."

I ran to the letter. Northern University was written on the

corner of the envelope. I almost gave myself a paper cut trying to open it. the letter read,

"Olivia Bailey, we would like to inform you that you have been accepted into."

I didn't even finish reading the sentence before I started to jump and shout. Granny came into the living room,

"What happened!"

When she read what I read she started to shout too. I ran to Pawpaw and told him, He smiled and said,

"Congratulations baby."

He kissed me on my forehead. I was so excited the next day; I couldn't wait to tell my people at school.

The next day at school I walked into my statistics class, we started class with our lecture, and in usual fashion our teacher Ms. Gee gave us some classwork. Afterwards, me, Brenda, and most of the class was done with our work. Soft conversations started around the room. I started to tell her about my acceptance letter. Before I could get the full story out, I heard Ms. Gee say,

"Olivia, I said no talking."

"Ms. Gee, we finished our work. I was just telling her about my acceptance letter."

Ms. Gee squinted her eyes at me and said,

"I don't care what you're talking about, I said be quiet."

Me and Ms. Gee had an issue in the past. I felt like she was singling me out. Today was the day for me. I was tired of being singled out by her. I wasn't even the only person talking in the room. I could understand if I was being loud, but I wasn't. I was tired of the injustice. I replied,

"Ms. Gee why you always singling me out?"

Ms. Gee pulled her pink slips out of her desk and started writing. I already knew what it was, so I started gathering my belongings. Ms. Gee held up the pink slip and said,

"Take this and get out my classroom."

I took the pink slip and slammed the door on my way out.

When I got to the Dean's office, my usual Dean was out of the office. I had to go to the only Dean that was there that day, Mr. Burlap. I instantly knew it was about to be some mess.

Mr. Burlap was the most racist Dean we had. He had been working at The school since African Americans were not allowed to attend. He would allow students to have lunch in his office, but only the Caucasian and Hispanic students. When it came to any other student, he was mean and surly. Every African American student that had him as a Dean always complained of his unusually harsh punishments.

When I got to Mr. Burlap's office, I handed him my pink slip and sat down. He read the slip, then pulled a suspension notice from his drawer and said,

"I see that you have had issues with this teacher before."

After he looked up my other write-ups from Ms. Gee. He continued,

"I'm going to give you a two-week suspension."

He held up the suspension paper to me. I sat there stunned. Graduation is in two weeks.

"Mr. Burlap if you suspend me for two weeks that means I won't be able to graduation."

He replied,

"Then maybe you should've thought about that before you decided to talk in class."

I slowly took the notice out of his hand and as I was walking down the hallway, I kept my hand on the lockers so I wouldn't fall.  My legs suddenly felt weak to me as I walked.  Right before I got to my locker, it dawned on me, I have an I.E.P. (Individualized Education Plan).

I was also assigned an I.E.P representative that I could talk to if I had any issues. I may not have known why I needed it but, I was well versed on what came with it.

When it came to my rep Mrs. Collier, I took one of her classes in my freshman year, so she knew how I was as a student.  I lifted my head up and wiped my tears. I ran to Mrs. Collier's class. When I got there, she was in between classes. Wont God do it!

I told her what happened from beginning to end. By the time I was done and handed her the notice she looked as stunned as I did in Mr. Burlap's office.

"He did what? Wait right here, don't you worry I got this."

Mrs. Collier walked out of the room like a melanated soldier on her way to battle.  While Mrs.  Collier was gone I called granny Odessa.

She said,

"He did what!"

I told her what Mrs. Collier said.

"Ok well let Mrs. Collier handle it, call me if she needs some

back up."

This was the first time that my granny didn't have to come up to the school. I was happy about it this time because granny had so much on her plate. I didn't want to add anything else. I prayed to God, asking Him to step into this situation.

When Mrs. Collier came back, she said,

"Ok I got the two-week suspension taken off. You will have to do a 3 day in-school suspension, but you will be able to go to prom next week and graduate the week after."

I broke down crying and calling on the name of Jesus. Me and Mrs. Collier Praised danced all through that classroom.

I went to prom the following week with one of my childhood friends. We had prom in one of the museums downtown. We partied like it was 1999, or whatever Prince said. But the main event was putting on my cap and gown for graduation. Lining up with my classmates, knowing that the enemy tried so hard to block me in so many ways almost made me shout going across the stage.

After everyone got their diplomas, they played Our graduation song 'on the ocean' by K'Jon. I got my diploma, and I went searching for Mrs. Collier. I didn't have to go far because she was searching for me too. I ran into her arms like I was just a child. I thanked her repeatedly as we cried together.

# Chapter 8

## STARTING SOMETHING

After graduation me, my family, and my friend from church, all went on a cruise. I was in the cabin with Mama, my sister Diamond, and my friend from church Erica. Soon as we got to our cabin our bags were waiting for us.

We freshened up from the long trip and hit the lido deck. I was so excited to be on vacation. Me and Erica walked the decks exploring the ship, we had ourselves a ball. We drank a few virgin pina coladas, ate at the buffet, and danced to the music. After we explored a little while longer, we decided to head back to the cabin to take a nap before dinner.

Our nap was interrupted when my mama burst into the cabin mad about something and started to curse me out for being in the cabin. I was every name, but the name God gave me, all in front of Erica. Erica looked shocked. My mama stormed back out of the cabin. I laid there staring at the wall with tears in my eyes.

I couldn't bring myself to say a word, I was so embarrassed. At this moment the saying, that's still your mother, granny Odessa always told me meant nothing.

I wanted to scream so badly, but I couldn't open my mouth. In my mind, I thought that maybe just once my mama could at least act like she loves me. Physically my vacation just begun. Emotionally my vacation was over.

I tried my best to be joyful for the rest of the cruise. Deep down I was just ready to go home. When we landed back in Chicago, Erica ran to her mom and hugged her so tight. That was the last time Erica went anywhere with me and my family.

While we were gone on vacation Michelle was trying to get in touch with me. She stated how she missed me so much and she still loved me. hearing that filled a void that I felt in my heart. I wanted to feel loved. I started to feel like I wasn't worthy of love.

So, when I saw the messages from Michelle, I jumped at the opportunity to feel loved. We talked and I forgave her and we got back together. Granny Odessa said after graduation I could date who I wanted since I was 18.

Me and Michelle were able to date openly. We wasted no time either. We enjoyed every bit of our freedom for the remainder of the summer. We went on dates, I would stay with her when her mom wasn't home, and life felt so good. We were excited about starting our college journey but hated the idea of separating.

Michelle got accepted into a university in southern Illinois. I was accepted into a university in norther Illinois. We promised to stay together when we got to college.

My time on the speech team inspired me to major in Theater Arts. I checked in on move in day. My family helped me move in. After we put my things down, we went out to eat and they dropped me off at my dorm room. We hugged and said our goodbyes then I watched them pull off.

I realized that for the first time in my life I was really on my own, I cried. I felt terrified. I didn't know how to handle my freedom. I didn't know how to adult. What was adulting anyway? I felt free, lost, happy, and petrified all at the same time.

The last couple of years since I came out to my grandma, she stopped teaching me life lessons. Pawpaw had Alzheimer's and was unable to teach me the way he used to. I felt as if I was up a creek without a paddle, left to fend for myself. I still didn't know how I would navigate this thing called 'life',

I laid down in my bed with the biggest smile on my face. I may have been afraid, but I was ready to see what life had for me.

The next day was orientation for all underclassmen. I showed up decked out in my red, black, and white. As we walked into the basketball arena and got to our seats, I was amazed at how big it was. Popular music was playing. We danced while we waited for the school President to give his speech. When President McGowan approached the pulpit, I settled into my seat ready to hear the most motivational speech I have ever heard. President McGowan started by saying,

"I would like to congratulate you all for being accepted into Northern University. I want you to enjoy yourselves, party, and have a good time. Welcome to NU!!!"

He then walked out of the arena. Everyone started to cheer.

I sat in my seat with a raised eyebrow. I thought, *that's it?*

I looked around and saw only black students in the arena. That's when it all made sense. He was motivating us to fail not win. I wasn't too surprised since I already knew how Illinois was when it came to racism. Racism was deeply engraved into Illinois' way of living. I was slightly annoyed, but I brushed it off as we left the arena.

On my way out of the arena, I saw some of my old classmates from many different stages of my life. I saw some people from my west Englewood days, my calumet city days, and even some people from when I went to that language academy off 95th. It felt so good to catch up with them and see how they were doing.

One of my old classmates introduced me to this guy named Terrell. We struck up a conversation and realized we had a lot in common with each other.

Terrell invited me to a kickback at one of his friend's house later that night. I happily accepted his invitation. We met up with a couple of other guys; Mark, Mathew, and Patrick on our way to make a stop at the gas station. When we got to the gas station, I grabbed some squares and Terrell grabbed some cigarillos.

We walked into the house and there were so many people there. Some people were in the living room smoking weed, I knew it was weed because of the smell. I was familiar with the smell of marijuana because my uncle would pick me up from school and his car smelled just like it. Back when we called it reefa. So, I was somewhat familiar with the scent of marijuana.

We turned the corner and there were some people in the dining room sitting around a table with a mound of weed in the middle of the table. It was so smokey in the house I was surprised the smoke alarms didn't go off. Mathew, Mark, and Patrick pulled a fat bag of weed out. I had never seen that much in my life. I guess it showed on my face because Terrell looked at me and said,

"We call this a session."

We sat down at the table, and they pulled out cigarillos and Terrell slid me a couple and that's when it hit me. I don't know how to roll.

I looked at what everyone else was doing and I mimicked their movements. When I was done, I joined in the session. We sat and listened to our favorite 90s rap and RnB songs, while we played some spades. The more I smoked the more I forgot about my problems and trauma.

I felt like nothing else mattered but the inhale and exhale of the blunt. I felt numb to the issues of life, it was an escape.

Then came the munchies. We left and headed to our dorm cafeteria and ate everything they had. It felt good to be able to escape the trauma that plays repeatedly in my mind. I don't know what that feeling was but I wanted to feel more of it.

# Chapter 9

NEW BEGINNINGS

Finding a place to smoke became a daily routine for me. It was all that I could think about when I woke up in the morning. Even in class I found myself thinking about when I would smoke again. I couldn't eat, sleep, or have fun if I hadn't smoked.

It got to the point were going to class was getting in the way of me smoking. I no longer wanted to write my poetry. I was hooked. Most of my friendships I gained was from us smoking.

We only understood each other when we were high. I stopped calling Michelle when I said I would due to me smoking.

One day, I called Michelle and some female answered the phone. I crashed out when I hung up the phone. I didn't answer when Michelle called back. Smoking weed became my new relationship. Before I knew it, I was only going to class to take tests.

I got a letter stating that I was being put on academic probation due to my GPA being 0.95. That was the lowest GPA I have ever had in my life. I was so disappointed in myself that I went to go smoke to escape it.

I didn't care about school anymore. I only cared about running from what I was feeling on the inside. I wanted to numb everything. If I wasn't high, I wouldn't be happy. I started to build a tolerance. So, I smoked more just to feel high again. I wasn't chasing the numbness anymore I was chasing the high.

I was proud to be a pothead. Being high became my identity. When I didn't have money to smoke, I started to sell weed to get the money.

When I got the letter saying I couldn't return to NU, I was too high to care. I still had weed so I was good. When my grandparents came to pick me up at the end of the semester.

Granny looked at me and said,
"Well, if you want to be a dummy, be a dummy. But when you get back home you gone work or go to school there is no in between."

That statement woke me up out of a deep spiritual slumber. I cried silently the whole way back home. I felt like the biggest failure in the world. I wallowed in self-pity for a few days. Oh, but when I woke up the next morning after them few days. I felt a fire burning inside of me.

I asked my grandma to give me a ride to the community college. When I got there, I registered for the upcoming fall semester. I took my placement test. I tested so high in literature that I didn't have to take literature classes. When it came time to start class, I hit the ground running. By the end of my first semester, I achieved a 3.0 GPA. When I showed my grandma my grades, she looked at them and said,

"ok"

I still saw the disappointment on her face. Enough was enough, For the first time in my life, I didn't care about getting validation from anyone but, God.

After finishing my pre-requisites, my first semester I signed up for an acting course. My professor's name was Roxy Waltz. She was a master of Her craft. The way She loved Acting and the way She inspired us was amazing. Her light shined so bright you had no choice but to get excited about what She taught. Mrs. Waltz saw something in me that I didn't see in myself. I truly enjoyed Her class.

I started to believe in myself a little more. I was starting to believe that maybe everything I was going through wasn't for nothing.

I started talking to this new girl named Honey Valentina. She was a couple of years older than me. We hit it off immediately, she was funny and beautiful. She was from Long Island. After talking for a while, we realized we had a lot in common.

After a few weeks of virtual dating. We made it official.

Me and Honey dated for a few months. Then I visited her, I found out she was living with her dad. She said they were struggling with paying bills and after a couple of visits she asked if I could move in to help. I didn't hesitate to say yes.

I was excited to tell Mrs. Waltz. She had become more than just my professor; she was every bit of a mentor.

"Are you out of your mind? You're just going to throw away your future like that."

I was so confused; I thought that since she was from NYC

she would be excited for me. I hated to disappoint Her, but I had to live my life. It was time to move to the Big Apple. It was time for a new beginning.

# Chapter 10

## NEW PLACE, NEW NAME

I was greeted by Honey at the airport when I landed in New York. She was so beautiful; I fell in love with her more every time I laid eyes on her. She was slightly taller than me with a body like a coke bottle. Her smile lit up the darkest of rooms. Her hair was long and soft. I felt ready to take on the world with her by my side.

We headed to their tiny and cramped apartment. I introduced myself to her dad, he seemed cool. He was a tall, husky guy who could make a mute person laugh. I affectionately gave him the name, Baldy, After our introductions. Me and Honey wasted no time hitting the town. I marveled at New York's beauty.

I felt like I was supposed to be there. I gave myself two weeks to get acclimated to my new home. During this time, we explored, went on dates, and just immersed ourselves in each other's company. After my two weeks were up, I started to put applications in for work. Honey had suggested I apply to be a direct support professional like her. She explained that She provided direct care for neurodivergent individuals who lived in group homes.

I applied and within a week I was hired as a direct support professional. I noticed that taking care of another person came natural to me. I began to love my job. I learned so much like how to properly provide care and how to handle everyday life at a group home. I loved the fact that you never knew how your day was going to go when you got to work. Every day was a brand-new day.

One night, Honey called her friend Bree and Bree' s stud girlfriend Riley. We all decided to head to a gay club in Manhattan This was my first time at a gay club. When we got to the club there was a stage in the middle of the dance floor set up for what Honey called a 'stripper show'. I had never been around so many gay people in my life. It took everything in me not to walk around with my mouth open.

I saw feminine women, masculine women (studs), feminine men, and masculine men. Honey informed me that some of the masculine men were transgender men. I asked what that meant, she said,

"It means that they were born woman but, they are transitioning to men now."

I didn't even know you could do that. It made so much sense to me. I didn't think too much about it as we sat down to watch the show. Later the topic stayed on my mind. My curiosity was in full effect.

Ever since that night I couldn't stop thinking about the trans-men I saw at the club. I had no idea that was something you could do. I already enjoyed being called male pronouns when I was with my bros. I also enjoyed being the masculine figure in my relationship. At first, I thought that it was just hyper masculinity.

The next day I began to study how I could transition. I made two appointments to speak with a doctor and my psych doctor for later that day. When I got to the clinic, after my telehealth psych appointment I was able to speak with an HRT. I had a 15-minute conversation discussing the pros and cons of testosterone. I signed a contract and headed to see my new doctor.

Me and Honey met with my new doctor when she got off work. I was so happy that she decided to come with me for support. Having her there helped to ease my nerves. We agreed to start with 1 ml injections every two weeks. I chose injections because they were the fastest way to get my desired results. After some training on the injections, I walked out of that office with the biggest smile on my face.

I fantasized about having a thick beard, no chest, and a deeper voice. I also researched the different types of bottom surgeries, but I chose not to put my body through that process.

I was so excited because I was on a road that felt good to me. On the ride home, Honey looked at me and asked,

"Have you picked a name yet baby?"

I thought about it for a second. Then I replied,

"Oliver Ezekiel Bailey"

She loved it and I did too. From that day forward I had a new name.

# Chapter 11

## WALKING SHELL

A month went by, and everything was good. I was happy to be taking the necessary steps to feel more comfortable in my skin. Except, I woke up extremely angry for no reason. I almost panicked until I remembered that T-rage was one of the symptoms of testosterone. Thankfully it didn't last long.

Things were going good at home, but the atmosphere at my job was starting to feel weird. I noticed that my manager Lisa was starting to become more and more irritable towards me. It was as if a switch flipped.

One day me, Lisa, and one of my co-workers were talking about our favorite foods. When it was my turn to share that my favorite food was fried chicken and fries with mild sauce.

Her response was,

"Oliver you're so ghetto."

I awkwardly laughed her response off because she was my supervisor, but it made me feel uncomfortable. For me, liking fried chicken wings with fries and mild sauce was not ghetto. I resented her systemic prejudice.

Fried chicken was created by African Americans and is one of the most loved foods in the world. Mild sauce is a staple of Chicago culture. My love for fried wings, fries, and mild sauce was way more than a stigma to me. That meal is a part of my culture. That was the day I started putting applications in for other agencies.

We had a BBQ at the group home celebrating its grand opening before our residents moved in. We all invited our family. Lisa invited her husband. Our regional coordinator Bryan was also in attendance at the BBQ. Everything was going well. We were having a good time.

We had the volleyball net up in the backyard along with some games going. When we walked outside to partake Lisa said,

"Hey baby."

When she said baby, both her husband and the coordinator answered, it was giving mess for me.

Me and my co-workers looked at her husband to see if he was going to catch what the coordinator said, but he didn't. Uncomfortable wasn't, even, the word.

A few weeks later, the work environment got a little better. It made me happy to see the smiles on our individual's faces. Working as a Direct Support professional in a group home changed my life and made me a better person. We weren't just there as staff. We were like their mentors. Their confidant. More times than a few, I learned more from my individuals than I could ever teach them. Navigating the good times and the bad times with our residents created a bond that I had never seen before at any job. I felt that I had found where I was supposed to be in life. Or at least that's what I thought. Just when things were going good again. Lisa began micromanaging every little thing I did. My workdays were becoming toxic and stressful.

I knew it was time to start looking elsewhere for work. I applied to the top agency in New York. I interviewed with them and was hired on the spot. When I went back to work. Lisa called me and asked me to meet her at the main office instead. When I got there, she fired me. I hated leaving everyone I bonded with in the group home, but thanked God for delivering me from Lisa's toxicity.

I started at the new agency that following Monday. I was so happy that my new supervisor Rick was an amazing supervisor. He was a good example of what it meant to work with passion and what it looked like to walk in your purpose. He saw something in me that I had no idea was there. Rick saw my passion, and he saw the light inside of me. Watching this transition in my life was so refreshing. Finally, I was being seen for who I was and not for the labels that others tried to put on me.

Unfortunately, my home life was transitioning as well. I noticed that Honey started to act differently towards me. She started to act like she was tired of me. At first, I thought it was because I was working too much. I was doing a lot of overtime at my new job. So, I scheduled more date nights on my days off. I thought that would help. I also noticed that she was getting close with her male co-worker. I didn't want to be that insecure boyfriend who couldn't handle their girlfriend having guy friends. So i didn't press the issue.

One day I got a message from a random girl on one of my social media platforms. She claimed to be the girlfriend of Honey's male co-worker. She informed me that Honey and her boyfriend had been sleeping together for months. As I read her words my heart sank into my stomach.

I confronted Honey about it, she became nervous and started to shake. She immediately denied it. The co-worker's girlfriend sent the screenshots. When I showed them to Honey, she knew the jig was up.

She finally admitted to cheating on me with Her co-worker. I stood still for a while, then I walked out the door. It wasn't until I got to my car that I realized that I had nowhere to go I had moved to a new state by myself. I had a good paying job but the rent was way too high for me to afford it on my own. I was up the creek without a paddle. I felt trapped.

Eventually Honey came outside to talk to me. With tears flowing down her face, she apologized to me. She said it would never happen again. She said how much she loved me and didn't want to lose me. I loved her but what she did was foul. I didn't know what to do. Shoot, at that moment I understood what the old folk meant when they said they were stuck between a rock and a hard place. I just kept thinking. *Why would she do this to me? Why does this keep happening to me? Is it me?*

So many things were flowing through my head. I felt exhausted. I got out of the car and walked back into the apartment with an overwhelming feeling of defeat. I decided to sleep on the couch. I had no energy to address any of the emotions in my head.

I didn't speak to Honey for a week. I only spoke when I was

at work. I started to feel angry with myself. Mentally I started to self-sabotage. I felt like I should've known better.

I retreated into my shell. I barely spoke to my family back home. I had no words to say. I felt stupid all over again. There were times like this where I missed the talks me and my Pawpaw used to have. I remembered him saying, *Remember who you are.* That was the motivation I needed; I laced up my bootstraps and stopped throwing a pity party for myself. I had to get my focus back.

Before I knew it, Thanksgiving came around. Late that afternoon, my grandma called and asked to speak to Honey. She didn't even like our relationship, so I was confused. Honey's face got serious, and she went to look for something in the bathroom. She comes back with my old inhaler and hands me the phone.

"Hey granny what's going on?"
"Baby, your Pawpaw went into cardiac arrest, I'm so sorry to tell you that he didn't make it."

The scream that escaped my lips was the most gut wrenching scream I have ever screamed in my life. I fell to my knees.

*My Protector.*
*My Provider.*
*My Hero.*
*Was gone.*

I never even thought about life without him. It had always been me, granny, and Paw Paw. He said I would give anything to hear his voice, when I fell asleep during one of his long-winded lectures. I thought he was just jaw jacking like the old folk did. I didn't think he was really going to leave me. Physically I was still alive, but emotionally, I was gone. I was nothing more than a walking shell.

# Chapter 12

## SHE IS NOT WORTH IT!

The next day me and Honey flew out to Chicago for Pawpaw's funeral. I was completely numb to the world. I didn't smile, I barely spoke to anyone. I felt like my world was crushed. Every inch of my being wanted to be anywhere else but in that car.

Pawpaw was laid in his casket in his gray suit, his low Afro perfectly trimmed, and his 'soul brotha' patch looking like it always had.

I felt like I was having an out-of-body experience looking at him in that casket. Pawpaw was the backbone of our family. He had a gentle and kind heart, but if he ever hit you with that, *Look here my man.* Then we knew he was about to stand on business. He only said it when the Marine in him was about to come out. He was the greatest example of what a father and husband were supposed to be. Having him in my life was such a blessing. I felt like all the air had been sucked out of the room. I don't know why I thought Pawpaw would live forever. To me he was invincible. So, seeing him in that casket was a reality check I wasn't ready for.

When we walked into the church for Pawpaw's funeral the next day. Realizing that this was the last time I was going to see him overwhelmed me. The entire funeral was a blur to me. Until my father came around to view Pawpaw.

Even though we had an estranged relationship, I forgave him. I realized i needed to forgive him for me, not him. I was even working on being cordial with him. When I hugged him. In that moment, I felt like a little girl who just scraped their knee falling off their bike and needed their father's love. As I hugged him, he said to me,

"I'm so sorry for your loss. He was a great father to you."

I just hugged him tighter; I appreciated him acknowledging that another man stepped in to raise his child. As they closed the casket on my Pawpaw for the last time, I cried my soul out. I realized that would be the last time I would ever see him again.

After the funeral I looked for my dad, so I could tell him that I loved him. I couldn't find him anywhere. We headed to the cemetery and buried my hero in style. In what felt like a split second me and Honey were back in New York. I appreciated her being there for me during a traumatic event in my life. We got back together, and it felt like we were falling back in love again.

I distracted myself with work. The days started to blend. There were times when I didn't know what day it was. I treated everyday as if it were just a routine. It was nothing special. I only cared about work. At work, it was like I came alive again. The world suddenly regained its color. It was as if life had meaning again.

One night during one of my overnight shifts, I video called Honey. She had on lingerie. I stormed out of the group home, got in my car and called Terrell. I told him what happened and let him know that I might be in jail later.
"Think about it, what if you go and they don't want you there."

He was right. Defeated, I sat in my car, and I cried. I felt like my world was falling apart. Every time I took one step forward; I got knocked 10 steps back. I tried to talk to Honey about how I was feeling when I got off. She responded by saying nothing happened. She called me insecure and sensitive. Shoot, by the time we were done going back and forth, I was the one apologizing for even thinking she would do something like that. I literally felt like I was losing my mind.

I didn't know what was real and what wasn't. I almost thought that I actually was insecure and sensitive. Our arguments got so heated that she told me about her cheating on me. Not to confess, but to unload her burdens on me. *She not even sorry.* Turns out that she had cheated on me with every man and female that said she was cute, both protected and unprotected. I was enraged. I punched a hole in the wall, stormed into the bedroom, and closed the door. As I sat on the floor, I felt a tangible pain in my chest. When I cried, I felt like my lungs had been crushed. Everything hit me all at once and let me tell you, I was… not… ready.

I guess I was crying too loud, because Honey blasted her music to drown out my sobs. Oh, did I forget to mention that she confessed all this as she got ready for a girl's night out. Yep, every bit of triflin. That's when I heard that still and quiet voice say, *Get up.*

The voice was still but behind it was an authority that I couldn't ignore. The voice was like the command of the alpha in a pack of wolves. A powerful feeling flowed through me that I had never felt before. I stood up, wiped my face, and I walked out the door with my head held high.

Even though my head was high, I still felt like a fool because I loved her. Then it dawned on me I loved her potential. I saw greatness in her. I saw who she could be. I turned a blind eye to who she was. I thought that maybe if I loved her with all my heart, she would love me back. I thought my love, though flawed, could change her. I also noticed that loving the potential of someone has been a pattern in my life. Whether it be with my mama, my Granny, my uncle, Michelle, and everyone else I ever loved. Pawpaw was the only one that never gave me toxicity when I gave him genuine love. That brought on another wave of tears as I pulled into the parking lot of my job. I missed my Pawpaw so much. I felt so alone.

When I got home from work Honey was waiting on me with tears in her eyes. When I walked through the door she dropped on her knees and sobbed. She apologized for what she had done. We got back together. Relationships all have ups and downs, right?

The next day, when I got to work my supervisor pulled me to the side,

"Oliver, you have showed great promise since you started with us. I would like to recommend you for supervisor training."

I thanked him with the biggest smile and let him know I would be happy to attend the training. *Maybe things are looking up for me, I hope so.*

I was so excited to tell Honey what my supervisor said.
"I HAVE BEEN A DIRECT SUPPORT PROFESSIONAL FOR 5 YEAR! I HAVEN'T HAD ANY SUPERVISORS RECOMMEND ME FOR TRAINING! YOU BEEN IN THE FIELD FOR ONLY ONE YEAR AND YOU GET OFFERED THE TRAINING?!"

I just stared at her as she sobbed. Next thing I know I'm consoling her. Like a… damn… fool, I know. She got herself together and rolled a blunt for us. While we smoked the blunt, I was conflicted internally. This was supposed to be a happy moment for me, and I felt robbed of it. I thought she would be happy for me. That was the first day that I started to pray against the relationship. I prayed to God without ceasing. Shortly after, me and Honey's relationship got worse. We took a road trip to Virginia to visit her family. While we were there, we talked to her mom about possibly doing a family cruise. Honey's mom loved the idea, and she began planning it.

About two weeks before we were about to leave to go on the cruise. Honey said that she spoke with her mom and her mom had suggested that the family cruise should only be the family. My feelings were hurt, but I didn't let it show.

Two days before Honey was set to go on the cruise, I asked Honey if I could use her phone to contact the weed man to re-up. While I was sending the text to him a text notification popped up on her screen, The text read,

"Good morning baby."

I asked her what that was about and the conversation turned into a big argument. She started talking to me like I was nothing. Like she never loved me. Her tone and choice of words was so disrespectful. She accused me of going through her phone looking for something like an insecure child. That's when the argument really got heated. Honey looked at me with pure hatred and said,

"That's why I'm taking him on the cruise with me and my family, and his balls are going to be knee deep in my mouth."

It felt like an 18-wheeler slammed full speed ahead into my stomach. I blacked out and when I came too, me and Honey were physically fighting all through the house. At some point in the fight, I picked up a knife and put it to her throat. Right before I began to slit her throat, I heard a still quiet voice say, *She isn't worth it.*

I came back to my senses. She wasn't worth it, and neither was this relationship. I packed my things in a bag and walked towards the door. I would rather be homeless on the street than to love someone who could take me out of my character. I was truly sick and tired of being sick and tired. That was the straw that broke the camel's back. As I closed the door behind me, Honey was on the phone with the police.

# Chapter 13

## CHAIN REACTION

I got in my car and the only place I could go was Honey's friend Sherry house. I told her what happened, and she let me know that it was ok for me to stay there. I called my supervisor who had become an amazing mentor to me, I let him know what happened and he advised me to turn myself in. I agreed with his advice and drove to the precinct and turned myself in.  I was angry that I ignored the signs earlier. *How could I allowed myself to go through everything I went through with her*. Every 'loving' moment we had was manipulation to keep me connected to her. *Honey never loved me.*

"Breakfast."

The CO said as They gave me an egg sandwich and a cup of coffee. Shortly after I was cuffed and shackled to a couple other women and transported to the courthouse for arraignment.

Afterwards I was released.

I walked out of the courthouse and sherry was waiting for me. I was exhausted physically, emotionally, and spiritually.

I informed My Supervisor Rick that I had been released. He let me know that the Higher Ups said that I needed to be placed on suspension until my case was resolved. He told me that I needed to focus on myself right now and that my job would be waiting for me when I'm ready. He was right, I just didn't want to admit it. I cared for everyone else with perfection, but amid caring for them I lost me.

By now Honey was on a cruise ship accompanied by the guy she cheated on me with. I had to block her from all social media because she was dragging my name through the dirt, while leaving out everything she did. She portrayed herself as the victim to all who would listen. I became the biggest villain in her story. What hurt was her boasting about how her new relationship was so much better than ours was. She paraded her new man around. She acted as if everything about him was better than me.

My depression got so bad that there were times when I didn't want to get out of bed. I barely ate. All I did was smoke weed, cigarettes, and drink. I barely showered. I literally was a walking zombie around the house. Sherry and her friends tried to cheer me up, but nothing helped. I was lost in my own mind daily. I was losing weight and drunk every night.

After a month Sherry kicked me out. I gathered what I could in my car and headed to a shelter. I spent the next couple of days wallowing in my own despair. I eventually got sick of myself. I forgave Honey and decided to move on with my life. I felt free, it was like the world regained its color again.

I became friends with a couple at the shelter. We were like

three peas in a pod. At night we slept with our cots together. We created our own little family. When the social worker told us she had found a transitional home for all of us, we were excited. We found out that we were all in the same room together. Things were finally starting to turn around in my favor.

We put all our resources together and bought food and stocked our cabinet. After dinner we all went to bed and slept like babies. One day I got a call from my peoples. She told me that her girlfriend had a seizure at the bus stop on the way to her job. She asked if I could pick her up from work and take her to the hospital. I hopped in the car and headed to get her.

I took them to the pharmacy so they could get her meds. When Shandrella got her girlfriend's meds, we got in the car and headed towards the exit. That's when I saw Riley walking in the parking lot. I hadn't seen her since we fell out a couple of months ago. Her mouth got too disrespectful. It was on sight at that point.

She looked at me and I looked at her with a grin. We already knew what it was. On sight means just that, on sight. She yelled out,

"Pussy!"

As soon as she said that I put my foot on the gas and watched her head crack my windshield. Shandrella and her girlfriend were screaming as she rolled over the top of my car. I was silent.

That was the last time I was going to be done dirty by anyone else. That was it, I lost control, I wanted her to feel the pain I was feeling inside. I glanced at her as she laid motionless on the pavement. I felt a sense of satisfaction. Yall gone learn to leave me alone. One way or another.

# Chapter 13

I had really lost it.

# Chapter 14

## THINGS ARE NEVER WHAT THEY SEEM

Shandrella and her girlfriend were still screaming. It was utter chaos going on around me, but I was eerily calm. *Why am i so calm, I just hit someone!* Yep, I needed to go to jail. I was reckless and dangerous. I was prepared to call the police at that very moment, but I didn't know if the officers would give my friends a ride home. So, I decided to try and get them back to the house first. As I drove off, I was followed by a man in a motorcycle. I paid no attention to the red light in front of me as I plowed through it. I also didn't pay attention to the four cars I plowed through as well.

When we stopped, I asked if they were hurt, and they said no. I had one scratch on my forearm. I apologized to the people I hit. I felt bad about hitting them. They had nothing to do with my anger. It was nothing left to do but … call Granny.

I felt like I was in the principal's office about to tell her I got suspended. *I'm more scared about her reaction then i am about going to jail.* I almost laughed out loud.

"Hey granny I just wanted to let you know I was in a car accident."

"WHAT! What do you mean you were in a car accident?"
"I'm ok don't worry but I need you to be strong for what I am about to tell you next."

I began to inform her that I was about to go to jail. When she started to become hysterical, I told her to be strong and that I would be ok. I couldn't tell her what happened because the police had just shown up. I learned from my last encounter with the police to be silent until I spoke with my lawyer. I reassured her and said I would call her when I was able to make a call. The officer instructed me to turn around. After he removed my items and handcuffed me, I was put in the back of a police cruiser.

When I got to the precinct, they put me in the interrogation room and left me in there for hours. As I waited, the room kept getting colder and colder.

"So, I got your friends side of the story. Do you want to tell me yours."

The detective said,

"I have nothing to say without a lawyer."

The detective then stormed out of the room and left me there for another 4 hours. He came back in and attempted to get a confession. I remained silent. When he left again, I put my feet up in his chair and took a nap. Ig…nor…ant. An officer came and uncuffed me from the floor shackle. He escorted me to a holding room where a couple of other people were waiting for transport. Another officer walked up to me and handed me a burger and a cup of coffee. Yea they were dead wrong for that. They tried to make me look like a snitch.

Shortly after we were transported to the courthouse, I was placed in the female bullpen. When it was time for arraignment, the Judge set my bail at $250,000. When it was time, I was loaded into a patty wagon and transported to the jail. Where I was processed and given my phone call. I called Granny Odessa. I let her know that I was ok and not to worry. After my call I was strip searched for the first time. After it was over, they gave me my county greens, a bag of toiletries, bedding, a blanket, and sent me back to the holding area.

We sat waiting to be escorted to our cells, when out of the vent, we hear a man grunting and moaning. The next thing we heard was,

"You fucking faggot!"

And more moaning and grunting. Then we heard the man sobbing softly. Me and the other inmates sat and just stared at each other with our mouths open. *Did I just hear a man get raped?*

A CO came to escort us. We grabbed a mat. They escorted us to the east block. We split up and half of us went to tier A and the other half went to tier B. I got to my cell. I was so exhausted, all I cared about was putting the mat down, making my bed, and going to sleep.

I dreamed that I was walking down a pitch-black road by myself. I heard a growl behind me. When I looked back, I saw a sea of red eyes and white pointy teeth running towards me. I took off running. A church with a huge bell tower came into view on the left side of the street. I ran into the church. When I ran inside there was a staircase. I ran as fast as I could up them stairs, one of the demons chasing me grabbed my foot.

I broke free. The stairwell was destroyed halfway up, I was almost trapped when I saw a broken wooden ladder that led up to the bell tower platform. In one effortless leap and in the same motion I took an effortless leap I caught the ladder with one hand. Before I could even be shocked that I made it, a group of demons jumped behind me and landed on the ladder beneath me. I kept climbing as fast as I could then suddenly the brightest light I had ever seen shun from the bell tower. It was so bright I thought it would hurt my eyes but instead it was warm, welcoming, and safe.

Out of the light I saw Pawpaw's arm reach down towards me. I immediately reached up and grabbed his hand. I was lifted onto the platform. I saw my Pawpaw's body, but I couldn't see his face in the light. *My Pawpaw* I just laid my head on his chest and felt peace that surpassed all understanding. I watched as he waved his right hand, and all the demons fell and were sucked out of the doors of the church. As the church doors slammed shut my eyes opened.

I guess if God wants to reach you, He will reach you wherever you are. God gave me a promise in my dream. I could feel it.

# Chapter 15

## NEVER GET TOO COMFORTABLE

A couple of hours after I woke up, I realized that the cell door hadn't opened. I asked the CO walking by why I was still in the cell. She yelled, "DO I LOOK LIKE A CLERK AT AN INFORMATION DESK!"

It took everything in me not to curse ole girl out. I was trying to figure out who she thought she was talking to, whole time. I swiftly had to remember where I was. The tier rep walked down to my cell and let me know that I was in 21 hour lock up and that I would be let out for three hours a day to use the phone, shower, and watch TV.

It took some time to adjust but I got the hang of it after a while. I got me a couple of books and a bible from the law library. Once I was able to keep my mind stimulated, those

21 hours became more bearable. Before long, I was moved to general population. They decided to house me in maximum security general population on the west block. One thing I had to learn about jail is I am in control of nothing. I was just happy that I wasn't in the 21hr lock up anymore.

I kicked it with a couple of people while playing cards. After finding out where I was from, they gave me the nickname 'Chicago'. One of the old heads gave me advice on how to deal with my case. They told me what law books to study from the library. Public Defenders, and what to do if you come across one that's not for you. This advice came in handy when my public defender told me,
"Just because you argue with someone doesn't mean you run them over with your car."
Needless to say, I fired him. He was right but he sounded like the D.A. The old heads taught me how to request an 18b lawyer which I learned was a paid lawyer that takes a pro bono case. My request was approved by the judge, and I was assigned an 18b lawyer. When I got back to the tier I called granny and let her know about my new lawyer. After congratulating me I asked if she could get a message to Tony.

Before I got locked up me and Michelle started texting. She apologized to me about how she handled me when we were together, and I apologized to her about how I neglected her during my time away in college. We agreed to be friends. I just had to call her and let her know I got locked up so she wouldn't think I ghosted her. Granny said she would get the message to Tony.

The next day I called Michelle, and she answered the phone. It felt so good to hear her voice. I let her know I was ok. I couldn't talk too much about my case on the phone. We talked for the length of the call. Michelle told me that she would put money on the phone and my books. She also said that she would write to me. The fact that she even wanted to support me touched my heart. That was one less thing I had to worry about. Now I could focus on doing my time.

I met a new friend named Macy. We became something like best friends. We would always crack jokes to make each other laugh. Shoot, we would have the whole tier laughing at our silliness. Once a week we would have movie night were we would all get our blankets, and our commissary snacks or whip ups we would make from leftovers, and watch whatever movie we chose to watch from the TV guide that was in the Sunday paper. Movie nights were our favorite nights of the week. Sometimes it felt like we were on the outside, the way we all sat together like a family. I started to pray more. We were learning about God and learning about how to live our lives for Him at church services on Wednesdays. Even the Cos noticed how close we were on the tier. This felt too good to be true.

We got a new girl. She just turned 18 and was moved from the juvenile tier. Her name was Justice. We immediately took her under our wing. She was in jail for armed robbery. We didn't judge her; we shared knowledge and advice with her as much as we could. We hoped that our knowledge would help her along the way. Justice quickly became well-liked by all of us. We treated her like family. So, it was a complete surprise to us when she woke up one morning and decided to pick a fight with me over the phone.

We all had time slots for the phone, and it was my time to be on the phone and she comes and tries to get on the phone during my time. That was a violation, I couldn't allow it. By this time, she knew that phone time was important to everyone locked down. I tried to be calm with her because she was young. But, a violation like that had to be checked. So I took the phone and hung up her call. Macy and a couple of other girls got in between us just as Justice tried to steal off me. At that very moment I forgot she was 18. It took four people to keep me from putting hands and feet on that girl.

The CO came in just before I could get to her. He locked the hold tier down, came to my cell and told me to roll up. I gathered my things and headed to the sally port. They moved me to the east block aka 21hr lock up. When I got over there the tier rep. Leala, put me up on game.

"Now she know she wrong for that, she did all of that just so she could get moved back to the east block so she could be with her girlfriend."

I was so mad I could spit fire. I had my people I was kicking it with, I had a great cell right in front of the TV. We were having a ball every day. That's when I learned my second lesson in jail. Never get too Comfortable.

# Chapter 16

A BIRTHDAY TO REMEMBER

When came out my cell the next day Leala came to talk with me. She told me she had a murder charge. We became cool. Leala even chose me to be the assistant tier rep. She was one of the sweetest and most God-fearing person I had met in jail yet. She became a mentor to me. On the days we went to court we would pray together. When the DA tried to give me six years in prison and three years on parole, we prayed about it and the next time I went to court I accepted a deal for two years in prison and two years on parole.

We celebrated and praised God as We sat down and ate dinner trays. The news began reporting on Leala's case. I knew she was being charged with murder. I didn't ask about the details. According to the news Leilani was accused of murdering one of her tenants, chopping her up. Spreading her body parts all over New York. I was shocked by the allegations, but I kept eating as if I heard nothing. I didn't ask any questions I just minded my business on that one.

Shortly after I signed my plea deal, Leala was given 45 to Life and immediately taken upstate. A week after Leala left, I was moved back to the west block.

They moved me to the tier where Macy and a couple of other old heads I knew were on. After saying hey to everybody and putting my stuff in my cell. When I walked back out, Macy called me over to play spades. I sat down with her, one of the old heads, and the new Hispanic woman that just moved onto the tier. Macy introduced us saying,

"Chicago this is Esmeralda; Esmeralda this is Chicago."

I noticed that shorty was cute.

A couple days later me and Esmeralda started flirting. I was flattered by her advances. I informed her that I had a girlfriend at home. She did too.

I was still on the fence. I loved Michelle. She was my first love, but I was really starting to like Esmeralda. Our flirting eventually led to a jailhouse romance. We didn't make it official, but people knew we were an item. I felt bad when I talked to Michelle on the phone, but I kept telling myself that I was just surviving, and I would tell her everything when I got out. *It's not cheating, it's jail...right?*

On commissary day before Macy's birthday me and a couple of the ladies on the tier got together at my cell and gathered what we needed for Macy's fat girl cake. And how we would celebrate her birthday. We decided to have a spades tournament and after dinner we would all sit in front of the TV and watch a movie. We had been planning this day for weeks. I even made a special batch of hooch. After getting everybody's contribution for Macy's cake I put the stuff in my box and we all locked in for count time.

The next day we woke up early and decorated Macy's cell with toilet paper while she was in the shower. When Macy got out, she was surprised to see her cell decorated. One of the girls kept Macy busy at the front of the tier while we were getting her fat girl cake together at the back of the tier. We started the cake off with a layer of crumb cake and brownie, then we topped that off with a frosting made from peanut butter, jelly, syrup, and hot chocolate. We crumbled some chocolate chip cookies on top of the frosting, then repeated the layers until we used all the commissary contributed to the cake. Right before lunch time we presented the cake to Macy and sang happy birthday. When we finished singing it was time for our lunch trays to be passed out. We ate lunch and all those that put on for the cake enjoyed a piece of it. After the cake we all chose our teams for the spades tournament. On my way to my cell, I saw Macy pop something in her mouth. I minded my business and continued to my cell to get ready.

We hit that spades table with a vengeance. We had six teams playing on the three benches we had on the tier. We played until we narrowed it down to the last two teams playing for $20 worth of commissary. The tournament came down to Macy, one of our old heads named Denise against me, and Esmeralda. We played best out of five and we were neck and neck. Macy and Denise ended up beating us by one book. It was a well earned victory.

After we all ate dinner, we took our medicine when the nurse came on the block. We all got our blankets and sat in front of Macy's cell to watch a movie with our cup of top-notch hooch.

*Fye, If I do say so myself.* About an hour into the movie the laundry was brought to the tier. As we all got up and grabbed our bags off the table, Macy was looking extra high. I told Esmeralda to stay with her and get her to drink some water while grabbed her laundry. By the time I grabbed the laundry bags I heard Esmeralda scream,

"SHE'S NOT BREATHING!"

# Chapter 17

## GRACE TO FREEZE

I took off running to Macy's cell and when I got there she was lying on the bed. Her face and lips was turning blue. I checked for her pulse, she didn't have one. I told Esmeralda to go tell the CO it was a medical emergency.

I pulled Macy down on the mat so her head would be flat. The mat was thin and on a steel slab, so I was able to proceed with CPR while she was on the bed. I began chest compressions. Everything that I had learned as a DSP came rushing back to me. When I got to the thirtieth chest compression, I grabbed a shirt from her laundry bag and created a barrier between her mouth and mine as I attempted to give her two rescue breaths. The first breath didn't make her chest rise. So, I moved the shirt and gave her mouth to mouth for two more rescue breaths. I watched her chest rise and started on my next set of chest compressions when I heard the Sargent,

"Lock in!"

I continued chest compressions while everyone else locked in. Then I heard,

"Bailey, lock in!"

"I can't stop CPR until someone takes over Sergeant!"

While I mentally kept count of chest compressions. He yelled for me to lock in again. This time I ignored him. I needed to focus, my friend's life was at stake. I finished my second set of compressions and started my second round of rescue breaths. *Come on Macy! You're not dying today!*

Just as I was finishing my third set of compressions, I saw something that I had never seen before in all the 10 months that I have been in county jail. A Sergeant walked onto the tier by himself without any Cos. The Sergeant walked into the cell and stood there watching me.

He just stood there. I got to the ninth compression of my fourth set before he finally took over. I walked out of Macy's cell exhausted physically and emotionally. I laid down on my unmade bed and just stared at the ceiling of my cell. After a couple of hours, the CO assigned to our block that night stopped in front of my cell and ask,

"Hey Bailey. You ok?"

I gave a week thumbs up as I continued to look up at the ceiling the rest of the night. At around 4:30am my cell door popped open. I came out and when I got to the Sally port the CO told me I was the new tier rep. I was surprised. Inmates usually picked the tier reps. I never saw a CO pick a tier rep before. I accepted the position and proceeded to pass out the trays.

Later that day we called a meeting on the tier. Everyone

agreed with the Cos choice for tier rep. We held a vote for the assistant rep position. Esmeralda was picked for the assistant rep position. After the meeting I went back to my cell and locked in. I had a lot on my mind. *I just want to be alone.* I made my bed and laid on top of it. I thought to myself, people always talk about how taking a life affects you, but nobody talks about how saving a life affects you. The anxiety that I felt after the adrenaline wore off was slightly overwhelming. It's like You play it out in your head over and over again, wondering if you did the steps right. You worry that your efforts weren't enough. The immense pressure that's on you to remember the steps to save a life in the first place. You try to overlook the fact that you saw someone that you were just laughing and celebrating another year of their life with, lying lifeless on their bed. A five-to-ten-minute encounter can really have a big impact on your life. I really needed time to process this. I trained for years to be ready for moments like this. *I wasn't ready.*

As the only trans man in the county jail, I had gotten used to being mocked. Especially when I walked through the main floor. Somebody always had something smart to say. I thought I would never stop hearing the wheezing sounds from that time I had an asthma attack after S.W.A.T. pepper spread a girl in the cell next to me that one time. So, you can imagine my surprise when we walked through the main floor towards the yard, and I heard complete silence. Then all of a sudden one of the Cos next to the bubble yells out,

"Good job Bailey!"

And started to clap. Next thing I knew the rest of the Cos stood up and started to clap for me. I stood watching with my mouth open for a second then, I said thank you and continued in line for yard. *Word travels fast.*

When we got to the yard one of the inmates from the east block let us know Macy was ok. They said the Cos thought she was trying to kill herself, so they placed her on suicide watch. We were so relieved to hear that she survived. We sent a message to her, and we all went back to the tier feeling much better.

The next day while I was in my cell reading a book, a youth educational program that would tour groups of school kids around the jail, was about to walk the west block. We purposefully tried to scare the kids as they toured, then they would choose a couple of inmates to go down to the chapel and share their stories with them. I would always ask if I could go down to the chapel to talk with the kids, but I never got picked. So, today we all just enjoyed putting on a show for the kids as they toured the block. When they left, our CO started to call off names to go down to the chapel. I heard my name. I was finally picked to go down.

I was so excited when I walked into the chapel. It was so hard to keep the smile off my face as we stood in front of the chapel. Each one of us, male and female, stepped up to tell our stories. Finally, it was my turn. I stepped up, opened my mouth to talk, and.......... I froze.

# Chapter 18

## GHOST TALES

After a couple of seconds, words finally came out. I started by giving a little bit of back story about myself. My message was about controlling your emotions. I explained to them how the lack of emotional control landed me behind bars. I was so happy to be part of something that could change the lives of many. After we finished, they gave us a plate of food from the CO cafeteria, and we went back to the tier.

From that day forward I had the biggest smile on my face that I couldn't hide. Being part of this program wasn't even about the plates of food for me. It was so much bigger than that. We had the opportunity to mold and guide the minds of the next generation. It was so strange how things were looking up for me while I'm in jail. In my mind, it was the last place I would expect the pieces of my life to begin to come back together. I got a job in the female property room cleaning and organizing all of the female property. I got another job cutting hair once a month in the barber shop/salon. My Goal was to stay busy.

I eventually got a new assistant rep named Neeka when Esmeralda was released. Everything was cool until we passed out lunch trays one day, I heard Neeka tell one of the other ladies on the tier that she couldn't have any milk. The lady she was talking to never bothered anyone. She would sit at the back of the tier and talk to herself. I stepped in the middle of them and told Neeka,

"Naw we not doin no bullyin, pick on somebody your own size."

As I picked up a carton of milk and handed it to the lady she was bullying. Neeka stepped in my face and said,

"Aint nobody scared of you Chicago."

Next thing I knew I was putting hands and feet on Neeka. We were moving furniture in that bad boy. I whooped Neeka from the front of the tier to the back of the tier. It was so bad that when the Cos came to break up the fight, I was the one told to roll up and Neeka was taken to the medical unit.

I went to my hearing. The hearing officer gave me 30 days in solitary confinement aka 'the box'. I was given two pairs of red and white striped jumpsuits and escorted to the box which was located on the east block. The box was a 22-hour solitary lock up unit. We had one hour at the yard daily and one hour to shower and make a phone call. We were still allowed to go to church, which I was grateful for. We were also allowed to go to the law library. I got a bunch of books from the library. I took the time given to me to just read.

I started writing poetry again. I had almost forgot that I even liked poetry, it had been so long since I had written a poem. It felt good to be able to express my emotions through the rhythmic metaphors that flowed through my pencil and onto the paper. Between writing poetry, reading my bible, and my books the 30 days in the box flew by.

At about 2am, a CO told me to roll up. I immediately knew what that meant. It was time to go up state. I gathered my things, leaving what was left of my commissary for whoever cleaned my cell. I got processed out at the female property room. Shortly after I was cuffed to two other inmates and placed in the back of a sheriff's car, on our way to the maximum-security female prison.

We pulled into the facility, I saw a girl sitting in one of the windows at the reception building. The girl was wearing a red, black, white, and gold plaid school uniform with a black sweater. She had on white lace crew socks and black oxford schoolgirl shoes on. She was writing in a black and white composition notebook with a number 2 pencil when she looked up at me as I walked into the building. I could see that she was in her late teens, with long black hair. Her skin was slightly melanated and her eyes were jet black.

After being processed in, I noticed that they gave us state greens to wear. The uniform they gave us looked nothing like what the girl in the window had on. I thought that was odd, but I just assumed she had a different uniform for whatever job she was assigned to and brushed it off.

Over 20 other inmates and I were escorted to the housing unit. The housing unit was a larger room with cubicles all over the room and in each cubicle, there was a bunk bed and a double locker. When we got to the unit it was mostly full so by the time, they got to me there weren't any more beds available in the main room, so I had to be housed in one of the two isolation cells. When I walked in, I was informed by the CO that the door was unlocked, I was able to move about freely just like the other inmates. She proceeded to tell me the schedule in reception. While the CO was talking, I put my stuff down. I walked over to the window and realized it was the same window I saw the girl in. I looked at the window seal and noticed that it was too narrow for someone to sit on.

I froze, my eyes widened, and a chill started to go up my spine. It felt as if all the hair on my arm stood up. That wasn't an inmate I was looking at in the window.

She was already dead.

# Chapter 19

ONE HELL OF A JOURNEY

Well, I'd say my first day in prison went rather well don't ya think? Nothing like a little paranormal activity to get the blood flowing. On a lighter note, I learned to adapt to prison life Quickly, the first week flew by. I had the routine down and noticed that more and more people were being moved to general population within the first week. I wondered why they hadn't moved me yet. Then I remembered that 'Hurry up and wait' was the motto in jail. I finally heard my name a month later. I was surprised that I wasn't taken to the general population building. I was cuffed and shackled to another inmate and led to a coach bus. They gave us a brown paper bag and loaded us onto the bus. We started our five-hour drive to the medium security prison.

When we pulled into the prison parking lot, we were taken

to a bullpen for intake. After about an hour I heard someone yell,

"YOU FUCKING NIGGER!"

I wasted no time letting her know her racist rhetoric would not be tolerated. I was highly triggered. We didn't play that Nigger shit in Chicago. That shit would've got a mug beat up or worse. I waited to see if she was going to swing. I silently hoped she would, but she sat back down. Ten minutes after I sat back down two high ranking officers from the mount of caucus, walked in the holding room and told me to come with them. They led me to this dark hallway. I stopped walking and demanded they tell me where I was going. To which they responded,

"We're taking you to where you're going to sleep tonight."

At the end of the hallway there was a medical unit. Straight ahead was a long room with hospital beds along each wall. The Officers led me to one of the two cells on the left side of the hallway. The cell had a hospital bed, toilet/sink combo, and a shower. The cell had two windows, one facing outside and one facing the dark hallway. I realized that they led me to a cell where they put inmates with infectious diseases. I was standing in a quarantine chamber.

Right before one of the officers slammed the cell door shut, he told me I would be here just for the night. He assured me that someone would come to see me in the morning then he closed the cell door. I watched as the officers walked down the eerily dark hallway. I glanced into the cell across the hall from me. It had a PVC pipe chair with blue mesh. The chair was placed on a two-step platform in the middle of the room with one single light on over the chair. The light cascading over the chair gave an almost ghostly glow to the chair and platform.

There were straps for a person's arms and straps for their legs. It looked like a torture chamber.

I backed away from the window. I began to pray that God would give me strength as terror began to creep up my chest. I kept replaying the promise God gave me back in county, *you just to be captain save-a-hoe.* I threw the dress they placed to the bed for me on the floor. I got in the bed and laid down. I looked at the ceiling and thought to myself.

"At least its just for one night"

I closed my eyes and drifted to sleep.

# Chapter 20

## MIND GAMES

The next morning, the C.O. assigned to me introduced himself as C.O. Taylor. I asked C.O. Taylor why I was being held in a quarantine chamber. He told me that he didn't know why. He said I was the first person he had ever seen in that cell. I appreciated C.O. Taylor's honesty, but he could've kept that last part to himself.

Taylor assured me that he would take care of me while I was there. He made sure I had everything I needed not to get bored.

I almost didn't notice that a whole day had past and no one come to talk to me like the officer said. *God, I know you will never leave me nor forsake me. If you are allowing this God, I know you have a plan behind it. I trust you. Trusting me with this. I pray this in the name of the Father, Son, and the Holy Spirit.*

I closed my eyes and slept like a baby.  When I awoke for breakfast C.O. Taylor checked in with me,

"I heard they were going to send a deputy to speak with you today."

"Good maybe they can tell me why I'm in here."

About ten minutes later, I heard Taylor rolling a T.V. in front of the door.  He then pulled up a chair and we watched T.V. together. After lunch, the deputy came to my cell.

"Hi Ms. Bailey, my name is deputy Vasquez. I would like to start by saying I don't know why you are in this cell, but I do know that we are trying to find housing for you. Once we find it we will move you to general population, we should have you moved no later than tomorrow."

As I watched Dep. Vasquez walk out of the cell, I felt a lot better knowing that they had a plan for me.  I almost forgot that my birthday was tomorrow.  It would be nice if I didn't have to spend my birthday in this cell.  I took a shower, grabbed my book, then nestled into bed.

An hour went by, and a nurse was escorted into my cell. She came to confirm some medical information with me. After the confirmation I asked,

"So quick question, when will I be able to receive my testosterone? I was supposed to receive my dose yesterday."

The nurse looked at me and laughed.

"We're not giving you testosterone."

She continues to laugh as she walks out of my cell. She didn't even care that it was a violation of my civil rights in the state of New York not to honor any prescriptions that I came into jail with.

The sound of my cell door closing rang loud in my ears. The sound was louder than ever before.

# Chapter 21

## FLEETING SATISFACTION

Happy 26th Birthday to me!

When C.O. Taylor came in with another inmate and my breakfast, I told him it was my birthday. He told me he was coming back with something special for my birthday. I laughed it off. I wasn't expecting him to bring me something. 30 minutes later, I heard my cell door open,

"Happy Birthday Bailey!!"

Taylor yelled as he walked into my cell with a cupcake from the mess hall and an arm full of magazines and two new books from the library. I had the biggest smile on my face, and I laughed from a deep healthy place. I thanked him as he walked back out my cell. I settled in to read a magazine. I didn't even care that I wasn't going to be moved today.

A different C.O. brought my breakfast. I asked him if I could use the phone. It's been four days now. I couldn't call before

I left for the draft, so I knew my family was worried about me. The C.O. let me know that he was about to leave for the day, but he would let the next shift know. The next shift C.O. Informed me that the officers that put me in this cell said I couldn't make any phone calls.

It felt as if all the blood was drained from my body. I felt cold. The terror I initially felt when I first walked to this cell crept back up my chest. The first thing that ran through my head was these people could kill me, and nobody would even know where I was. It was like a fighter woke up in me and I looked that C.O. straight in the eye and said that I will not eat any food until I am able to call my family.

I refused lunch and dinner. About an hour after dinner the C.O. came back into my cell and said I could make a phone call. I hurried to the phone and called my granny Odessa and I told her everything that had happened since I been there. I gave her instructions on who to call. When I hung up the phone, I felt a lot better. I went back to my cell and settled in with my book. *At least they know where I am.*

# Chapter 22

## THE HARDER THEY FALL

Around lunch time of the fifth day, Dep. Vasquez was escorted into my cell. I listened to her tell me how they were still looking for a place for me in general population. She assured me that they would move me tomorrow. As she talked, a saying that old folk used to say back in Chicago popped into my mind, *She a lie and the truth ain't never been in her.*

By now I had accepted the fact that I would just be here until they let me out. Thank God for C.O. Taylor. When I felt like I was at my lowest, he was right there encouraging me to be strong. C.O. Taylor made sure that the one outfit I had been wearing since they put me in here stayed clean. He made sure I wouldn't be bored. He even went out of his way to make my birthday special.

It still baffles me how God keeps his hand on me. I was made to believe that I was an abomination, and God would never love me. What I was told and what I am seeing are two different things. God has kept his hand on me this whole time. For every demon God already had an angel in place. God loves me. Even me.

The next two days flew by. Before I knew it day seven had arrived. After Breakfast, my cell door flung open. Another C.O. stood in the doorway and said,

"let's go, you're going on the draft."

Immense joy came over me. I rushed to get my shoes on. As I attempted to walk out of the cell I noticed that the C.O. didn't move aside so I could exit the cell. Instead, he positioned himself in the doorway defensively and said,

"Don't walk up on me, that's the quickest way to catch an elbow."

I realized he was baiting me to say something so he could harm me and say I assaulted him. This C.O. had to be about six foot one and no less than 280lbs. You could almost feel his rage radiating off him. I heard the Holy Spirit say, *Peace be Still.*

It was as if Holy Spirit kept my lips sealed. I stepped back and looked him Square in his eyes and said nothing. I kept his gaze, while widening my stance subtly. I knew if he wanted to harm me he could, but I have never been one to back down from a fight. He was going to know he fought me, win, lose, or draw. He stepped towards me. I steadied myself and prepared for impact. I kept hearing what granny Odessa taught me growing up.

*"Baby, the bigger they are the harder they fall."*

# Chapter 23

## PEACE THAT SURPASSES UNDERSTANDING

We stood there staring at each other. It was just like the old folks would say, *You could hear a rat piss on cotton.*

After what felt like forever, the C.O. finally stepped aside and allowed me to pass. When I stepped outside it was a beautiful sunny day. I could even hear birds chirping. I took the deepest breath of my life. This was the first time I had stepped foot outside in seven days.

While they cuffed and shackled me, I asked if they had the rest of my things that I came on the draft with. The C.O. cuffing me said that my things never left the draft bus.

They finished shackling me to my riding mate and we sat down on the bus. My riding mate said,

"You're Bailey, right?"

I confirmed, With a confused look on my face. She then said,
"Yo! we heard about you"
Now I am even more confused. She continued,
"The C.O.s were talking about you, word to my mutha. Some were laughing about them having you in that quarantine chamber. They were saying that they should ship you off to the male facility. But deadass some of the C.O.s said that what they did to you was foul."
*Am I hearing this correctly?* She continued,
"Yea and other inmates were talking about it too. Especially the women that delivered your meals. Happy belated birthday by the way. I've been hearing about you all week. You gotta tell me what happened to you."
After I picked my mouth up off the floor, we proceeded to talk about what happened to me for the rest of the ride back to the maximum-security prison.

This shocked me. I became comfortable with being mistreated. It was as if all I knew was to endure and keep going. I hadn't talked about my pain since i was a teenager. I didn't think anyone cared really.

They took me to general population. I was in awe when we got to my unit. There was a stove top! I realized that it had been over a year since I had seen a stove top in person. I almost cried. The unit also had a rec room and a T.V. room.

I stepped into my cell and put my stuff up. I laid on the bed and exhaled deeply. For the first time in a long time, I felt peace. I thanked God for that peace.

# Chapter 24

## IT'S TIME FOR JUSTICE RIGHT?

I was in my cell less than 20 minutes before I was called to the administration building. I was scheduled to meet with one of the deputies named Dep. Johnson. When she called me, I thought to myself, dang she fine!

Dep. Johnson looked like that princess from one of the movies I used to watch as a kid. I can't remember the name. She was so dog on fine I almost forgot to speak. It wasn't until she said,

"Bailey, did you hear me?"

That I snapped out of my daze and said,

"No, I didn't. I'm sorry."

Dep Johnson chuckled slightly. Then I saw the wedding ring on her left hand, and I got myself back together. Dep. Johnson continued,

"I said I wanted to know what happened to you at the other prison? I received a call from the Deputy there and when your name was brought up something didn't sound right. When I asked where they were holding you, she couldn't give me a straight answer. So, I told them to send you back here. What really happened?"

I wasted no time in telling Dep. Johnson everything that happened to me. When I finished, her face became very hard and serious. Then she said,

"Come with me."

She took me to an office with a sign on the door that read, *Grievance Officer.*

"Mr. Towns, this is Bailey. Bailey, I want you to tell him what happened."

I told Mr. Towns what happened. He looked at me for a while. Then he said,

"I'm sorry that happened to you. Are you familiar with the grievance process?"

I informed him that I read about it in the rule book they gave us in reception.

Together Mr. Towns and I filed a grievance against the medium security prison. We filed based on unlawful holding and a violation of my constitutional rights concerning the administration of my medication, phone calls, and my right to have recreational time outside for one hour a day. I gave my statement on the matter and Mr. Towns emailed deputy Vasquez for her statement.

"Ok, the grievance process is complete I will call you down when I hear something back."

In my heart I could do a back flip. All I could think about was that I was finally going to get justice. I smiled from ear to

# Chapter 24

ear on my way back to my unit. Justice……. Finally.

# Chapter 25

P.H.C


The next day I was called down to Mr. Towns' office. "Hey Bailey, so I heard back from Dep. Vasquez. She stated that you were never housed in a Quarantine chamber. She said you were held in reception until you were drafted back here."

If smoke coming from someone's ears was a literal thing, you would've seen a cloud leave mine.

"So, they lying."

Mr. Towns told me that it was time to take it to my lawyer. He also gave me some information about a couple organizations that represent inmates who have been abused while incarcerated. I brushed the slight feeling of defeat off as I walked back to my cell.

As soon as I got in my cell, I got my notepad, pen and began writing my letters to each organization. There was no way I was going to let them get away with this.

I called my grandmother to see if she could call my lawyer. She let me know she had been calling him since I called her at the other prison. She informed me that he was no longer taking her calls.

"It's ok, I sent out letters to all the organizations Mr. Towns gave me. Someone will help with this."

I tried to focus on other things while I waited to get a response. Compared to the county jail, upstate was like a college campus. Although it was still prison at the end of the day, there was so much more to do. They had jobs, programs, a recreational gym, and even a school where inmates could get their G.E.D and take college courses. You could literally come into prison with no degrees and leave with multiple.

I started to get cool with some people. We would play softball in the yard. It was like a whole new world. It was a nice break from the frustration that I felt. One Thursday after playing softball in the yard we had a shake down. I had been upstate a month now, so I had kind of gotten the 411 about the C.O.s by now. *411? dang I'm old.* Some were cool, and others were butt-faces. There was one C.O. named McDonald that had a reputation for targeting masculine inmates. Almost everyone that warned me about this C.O. told me to stay away from her, don't argue, just do what she says and stay quiet.

So, as the C.O.s hit the unit for the shakedown, I saw that C.O. McDonald was with them and I knew it was gone be some mess. She would go out of her way to antagonize transgender inmates. She hated us the most. She always wanted to provoke us to say something so she would have a reason to lock us in our cell in a disciplinary action called preliminary hearing confinement or *P.H.C.*

McDonald and the other C.O.s walked on to our unit with their Sargent. They locked us all in our cells and they let us out one by one to shake it down. When they opened my cell the first person, I saw was C.O. McDonald. I almost rolled my eyes when I saw her. I just knew she was gone be on one with me. I stepped out of my cell and stood silently as McDonald and another C.O. tore my cell from the rooda to the tooda. When they were finished McDonald looked pissed. She came out of my cell mean mugging me. I guess she was mad that she didn't find anything.

McDonald continued to glare at me. I was never raised to cower away from anyone, so I quietly kept eye contact. McDonald then stepped towards me until we were face to face.

"You looking at me like you want to fight me or something."

I knew she was baiting me. I remained silent as two other C.O.s came and stood on either side of me pressing my back against the wall. I calmed myself and maintained eye contact.

"Do something, I dare you. Give me a reason."

She whispered to my face. The stare down between us was intense.

"Oh, you think you tough huh?"

She gave a maniacal grin, stepped back so I could lock back into my cell. As soon as my cell door closed, I heard C.O McDonald yell to the bubble.

"Cell 15!, P.H.C.!"

# Chapter 26

## BLACK STATISTIC

I t took everything in me not to curse her out. I knew that would only make it worse. After I cleaned my cell I laid down and started reading one of my books to calm my nerves. *It's ok, I'll plead my case at my hearing. I literary said nothing to her. There is no way this ticket can stand.*

I was Pre-hearing confined for 15 days. After a brief period of adjustment, I found my peaceful center in my cell. With everything that was going on around me. I picked up my notebook and began to write from my heart. Just as I finished the poem. My cell door opened,

"It's time for your hearing."

The C.O. said. I walked to the administration building ready to fight the powers that be. I wasn't guilty of what I was accused of, and I just knew I was getting out of P.H.C today with time served.

I presented my case to Lieutenant Daniels as if I was that famous lawyer from the Civil Rights movement, think his last name was Marshall or something. I'm talking big attorney energy. When I was done, I waited for Lt. Daniels to determine if I was guilty or not. I was innocent so I just knew I would hear her say Not Guilty. Lt. Daniels wrote some things down and looked up at me and said,

"I Lt. Daniels find you guilty and I sentence you to 30 days in keep lock."

# Chapter 27

## DOUBLE MIND

I just couldn't believe what the Lt. said. Even after all the evidence. Per the directives I could use video evidence to help plead my case. I had the clip of the incident presented in the hearing. So, hearing her say anything other than Time Served baffled me.

When I got back to my unit, I saw that C.O. McDonald was our C.O for the night shift. I refused to give her the satisfaction of seeing me mad. I straightened my facial expression and quietly walked to my cell. When she didn't open my cell so I could take a shower, I wasn't surprised.

One of the greatest lessons I had to learn was every battle was not my battle to fight. I still knew it was nothing but God that allowed me to keep my composure. She could take my freedom, but she couldn't have my joy.

I awoke to my cell opening for yard the next morning. As we walked to yard, I noticed this tall, curvy Latina inmate. She had long thick wavy black hair. I was captivated by her beauty. While I was looking at her, we caught each other's gaze. She smiled at me, and I knew what it was. I walked over to her,

"Hey beautiful, what's your name?"

She smiled bashfully and said,

"My name is maria, what's your name?"

Her smile was so beautiful I almost forgot to answer her,
"My chosen name is Oliver, but everyone calls me 'Chicago'."

Our conversation flowed from there. It was like reconnecting with an old friend. We almost didn't even hear when the C.O. called us to line up. We said our goodbyes and agreed to meet in the yard the next day. I found myself already looking forward to it.

I had mail when I got back to my unit. It was a letter from Michelle. My excitement instantly turned to regret as I read her letter. I was reminded of how Michelle was the true love of my life. I tried not to feel it though. Those emotions were dangerous.

Longing to be with Michelle could land me in a turtle suit. I loved her so much. But I knew that if I didn't adapt to life in prison that longing, would affect my sanity. I had to find a way to make it through my time. I hated it but it was necessary to survive. I knew when I got out, I was going to tell her about everything I did to stay sane. Our bond was tight, she would understand…I think.

At least that's what I kept telling myself to subdue the guilt I felt. She didn't deserve that. I couldn't focus on those feelings though. I had to survive. I grabbed my notepad and I wrote Michelle a letter and laid down. In the back of my mind, I looked forward to seeing Maria in the yard tomorrow.

# *Chapter 28*

## NEW BEGINNINGS, SAME OLD SONG

**M**e and Maria started what I called a 'yardmance'. We wrote letters to each other to read when we got back to our cells. Before I knew it, my 30 days were up. She still had 10 more days left so I made sure to send my letter through one of the other keep-lock inmates. When she got out of keep-lock we was stuck together like glue.

All movements, except for programs and work, were an opportunity for us to spend time together. We were like peas and carrots.

Time started to fly by. I saw that mugs were smoking weed and I wanted to make some extra money. So I hopped off the porch. I would sell what I had, re-up and keep pushing it. I became the Weed man.

One afternoon I was in the yard playing football. Right

as I was catching a fastball, I twisted my ankle pretty bad. Surprisingly, It didn't hurt as bad as it looked. I give the credit for that to adrenaline.

They took me to the medical unit. As soon as they looked at my ankle, they prepped me to head out to the male facility to see their specialist. Right as I was about to get strip searched I remembered that I still had two baggies of weed on me that I hadn't sold yet. When the C.O. found it, I already knew what it was. She looked at me and said,

"You know you going to S.H.U. right?"

# Chapter 29

## BREAKING MY HEART

All I could do was nod my head and just pray that they took their precious time with the transport. I was going to enjoy every minute of this trip. Twisted ankle or not.

I tried my best not to overthink it. At least I got to see the outside world today. I savored every moment of this transport. The one thing I could say about upstate New York is the scenery is beautiful. Not to mention, the male facility we arrived at was set in a valley with beautiful mountain like hills around it. It was almost the most beautiful place I had ever seen. I took a minute to take it all in as we drove past the barbed wire.

The doctor's visit went way too quickly in my opinion. I jokingly asked the C.O. on the transport to drive slow. They laughed and slowed down. Word traveled fast, the C.O.s transporting me knew I was headed to S.H.U.

When we got back, they processed me back in and took me to another bullpen where two officers came and attempted to question me. They wanted to know where I got the weed from. I told them I found it in the yard. After they realized I wasn't a snitch, they called for my escort to the Special Housing Unit or (S.H.U.).

My escort came to get me. On the way to S.H.U. the C.O. said,

"Don't trip, keep your head up. You gone lay down for a little bit, but you got this."

I nodded and told him,

"I'm ready."

I almost smiled, this moment was definitely giving 'Godfather' vibes. We got to S.H.U. so I could get processed again. As I was getting processed, in walks Dep. Johnson. She tried to get me to tell where I got it. I reiterated that I found it in the yard.

"You know you gone have to lay down for this right?"

I smiled and nodded my head.

I finished changing into my S.H.U. uniform. They cuffed me and shackled me just like they did on the draft bus. They then escorted me to my cell. My cell was surprisingly bigger than my cell in the uppers. There was a standard toilet and sink combo, bed, and a concrete table coming out of the wall next to the bed. I was so astonished by the size of the cell I almost missed the dress and panties they put on the bed for me to wear.

"I'm not wearing that. As per directive 18.3 I have the right to be provided with boxers and pantsuit pajamas. Is there a way I can receive those items?"

The C.O. looked at me, laughed and walked off. As a protest I decided to get butt naked and put the robe on. I figured eventually people would get tired of seeing my naked behind in this robe. I laid down after making my bed and prepared for sleep. I waited to see when the lights were going to be turned off, but only one of the two lights was turned off. After the long day I had I was too tired to care about the light. I fell asleep fast.

The next morning, I was able to go to the law library. I grabbed a couple of books, magazines, a notepad, pencil, and envelopes. I was escorted back to my cell. I read one of my books until dinner came. As I started to eat I noticed a little chemical flavor to the food. I just figured it was because it was the first time I ate jail food without sazon. About an hour later I noticed a pain in my chest. I thought it was just heartburn or gas. I figured I would just lay down and call it a night. I thought maybe my chest would feel better in the morning. Two hours into my sleep the pain got worse. I thought to myself.
"This don't feel like no heartburn. It almost feels like a...a...a
heart attack"

# Chapter 30

## DR. FEEL GOOD

I got up and called for a C.O., I told them my chest hurt. They cuffed me and took me to their makeshift medical unit. They called the Sargent on duty and reported it to him.

"Why did you take so long to report this. Write her up for not reporting a medical emergency."

I almost side eyed that man as I realized the back handed attempt to use directive 5.4 against me.

"I assumed it was heartburn, so I didn't report it as per directive 5.5 all false reports are subject to disciplinary action. I didn't want to report a heart attack, and it turned out to be gas."

*Thank God I read that rule book.* That man was trying to give me more time in S.H.U.

They escorted me to the main medical unit. Nurse Grimes hooked me up to the EKG again and saw that I was indeed having a heart attack. They took me to a transport van and rushed me to the hospital. We waited in triage at the hospital for 6 hours before they told us that we had to go to another hospital.

We made it to the second hospital, when we got there, they took me straight to an elevator. When we got to the top floor the doors opened, and I felt like I was back at the prison. We had stepped into a sally port. There were steel bars everywhere. Once I got into my room a nurse came to let me know that I wouldn't be able to see a doctor until tomorrow. They gave me some medicine to regulate my heart.

After the pain subsided, I settled in for the night. The room looked like a regular hospital room complete with a hospital bed, bathroom, and television. I was grateful to have a T.V. to myself. I took full advantage and watched it until I fell asleep.

Dr. Matthews woke me up the next morning. He explained that my blood pressure and heart rate were better. He informed me that my heart was having palpitations, so he wanted to run some tests.

"I'm going to keep you for a couple of days for observation. Then you should be set to go back."

I thanked the Doctor as he walked out. For the first time in my life, I was happy to be in the hospital. TV, comfy bed, beautiful view. And to top it all off great food. This was like a blessing in disguise.

I soaked up every minute of every day that I was there until I was discharged. They transported me back to prison. I assumed they would take me back to S.H.U., but instead they took me to the upper-level medical unit. They said they wanted to observe me some more. I was perfectly fine with that. The cell I was in was huge. It even had a shower in it. I asked for a book when the C.O. brought my lunch. By dinner I enjoyed a good read and relaxed.

Who knew a heart attack could feel so good.

# Chapter 31

## GET IT BACK IN BLOOD

They kept me for a few days for observation. When I was escorted back to S.H.U. I saw a five pack of boxers, two pajama pantsuits, and a ticket for trying to make hooch. All neatly laid out on the bed waiting for me.

I had my hearing two days later. My hearing was held with Lt. Daniels and a captain I never seen before. They began to inform me that when they were cleaning my cell, they found a cooler with fruit and water inside. After reporting their findings, they gave me the opportunity to give a statement.

I explained to them that I had received the fruit in a care package from home. I placed the fruit in the cooler with ice to preserve it. I also reminded them that I have been away from my cell for almost a month now, so the ice melted. I let them know that the fruit was for consumption not to make hooch.

My statement was followed by the captain stating,
"In my 20 plus years of experience, I believe the contents of the cooler were being used to make hooch."
The Lt. then sentenced me to 30 days keep locked in my cell after I am released from S.H.U. I wasn't too shocked about getting 30 days from Lt. Daniels, that started to become a routine with her.

I finished my time in S.H.U. and was moved to my new unit. I wrote to Michelle about what was going on. Maria also sent messages through people. When she found out I was in keep lock for 30 days, she got a ticket for something minor so we could have yard together. The sentiment was sweet and twisted at the same time. A lot of people sent messages to me giving respect for not snitching. I knew a couple of people on the unit, and they slid me commissary to hold me over. A couple of people even sent me a couple packs of squares.

Even my favorite 'OG Ole Head' Ms. Perry, came to visit me. I always loved her visits in my last keep lock. She had been down over 20 years and she always saved some knowledge for me when she came around.

Ms. Perry's wisdom was so refreshing. She sold body oils; we always had this on-going joke that she would give me one for free one day. I would always try to convince her, she would laugh and tell me no. It seemed like she really cared. I don't remember if I ever told her, but I cared about her very much.

One day Ms. Perry asked me to write a character reference for her upcoming parole hearing. I was so excited that I wrote it and had it ready for her by the next day. A couple days after her hearing she was approved for release. She didn't even have to be on parole. We shouted together when she told me the news through the door. We praised God for her blessing and said our goodbyes. God is so good.

About a week or so after me and Maria got out of keep lock, I got word that another 'Ole Head' named robins, copped from one of my people and didn't pay. Since she lived in my unit I knew what needed to be done.

Robins and I used to be cool. We always seemed to end up in keep lock at the same time. Robins was about 55 years old and stood about 6'2" and around 350 pounds soaking wet. Robins was also what we called a career criminal. She had been in and out of prison since she was 18 and she acted like it. She was serving time for murder. She always talked tough to keep the young ones in line. I heard through the grapevine that she always kept a lock in a sock on her to make sure that they stayed in line.

So, because I had shared a couple laughs with her, I decided to approach her cordially.

"Hey robins when you gone pay that 5 packs you owe.?

Robins looked at me up and down and said,

"I ain't paying nothing. Yall gone have to get that back in blood."

I looked at her silently and walked away. I was disappointed because I didn't want to take this to the next level, but now she is forcing my hand. I got word to my people letting them know that she was still refusing to pay. The decision was made, after my next commissary run, I had to get it back in blood.

# Chapter 32

## NEVER AGAIN

I did a big commissary buy. I made sure I was fully stocked on everything. After I put my stuff up I put my gym shoes on and went to go do what needed to be done. Now I'm only about 5'3" and about 180 pounds, but I'm fearless. I gave Robins one last chance.

"Hey, you got those 5 packs?"

Robins looked down at me and said,

"I told yall, get it back in blood."

Before she could get all of the word blood out, I jumped up and punched her right in her mouth. I kept punching with all I had. I was giving all face shots at some point I blacked out and just enjoyed the feeling of my fist hitting her face. I didn't even feel her hit me in my head with the lock in sock. I kept

throwing haymakers until I heard the C.O. yell,
"Bailey stop!"
While they cuffed me, I heard another C.O. say loudly,
"Now that was a fight!"
They took me to the medical unit. I didn't even know I had a golf ball sized knot on my head until the nurse told me it was there. A few minutes after my exam a Sargent walked in.
"Yea, really cool beating up on old people."
Although he was one of her friends, the words humbled me. He was right. I almost got mad at Robins all over again. *Dog on fool, all she had to do was pay up.*

They sent me to the medical unit and sent Robins to S.H.U. because she had a weapon. When I got back I was definitely P.H.C'd. Although I got a lot of clout from that fight, I kept playing what the Sargent said to me in my head. I didn't want to fight her.

My hearing was quick, of course I was given 30 days behind the door. When I got out me and Maria got into an argument in the yard. We saw each other again at lunch and she carved *Chicago* in her arm. That was a bit much for me. We stayed friends though. Nothing more.

I was jail single for about a week, before I hooked up with this girl named Porsche. She could cook and I had commissary. The best part of my day was still talking to Michelle. Her letters kept me going, I had to push aside my feelings of regret. I just knew she would understand when I told her everything.

I got a letter one day from one of the organizations I wrote concerning what happened to me at the medium security prison. They informed me that my treatment wasn't severe enough for them to represent me in this case.

I ripped up the letter and locked in for the day. The next day

I got another letter from the parole board stating that my early release was denied. I was denied due to the number of tickets I received. *At least I got to talk to my lil cousin for his birthday in two days.*

I kept thinking I got to be strong for him. He was my little man.

Two days flew by. I walked out to the rec room to watch some T.V. movement had just been called, when this girl came onto the unit. She was mad about what we were watching. She began talking to me aggressively and loud. I quietly told her,

"If you trying to fight, meet me in the shower room."

But instead, she wanted to get loud. At one point she stood up and prepared to fight me. Just before we got to throwing blows, the CO stepped in between us and PHC'd us both. When I locked in, that was the first time that the walls felt as if they were closing in on me.

When I asked the CO if I could make a phone call, she told me no.

I instantly thought about my little cousin waiting for my call on his special day. I felt helpless. It was like the straw that broke the camel's back. I grabbed my state boots, removed the laces, and tied one end on a coat hook and the other end around my neck. This was it. I asked God to forgive me, as my body went limp.

# Chapter 33

## AYE DON'T COME BACK

When I opened my eyes gasping for air, I was lying on the floor in my cell. I heard a CO say, "Take her to OB."

OB was the suicide watch unit. They told me to strip when I got there. They gave me a green smock aka 'turtle suit', paper shoes, and escorted me to what looked like a Plexi glass cube. I was given a big thick blanket to sleep with on the bare stained mattress. A CO was assigned to watch me 24/7. When I needed to bathe, I was given a paper towel and a ramekin of soap. I washed up in the sink. Just like in S.H.U the lights never went off. They observed me for 72 hours then released me with an appointment to see a therapist.

"Do you feel depressed?"

"Are you feeling suicidal?"

I answered the Therapist's questions and then he sent me

on my way. I had so much that I needed to talk about. I felt like no one cared at all. Except Michelle, she made sure I knew she loved me, and I appreciated that. I finished my umpteenth keep lock bid. Porsche was released while I was keep locked so, I was back being jail single.

I called Michelle as soon as the phone was free. When she answered the phone, I was expecting a loving greeting as she usually did. When she answered the phone, she let me have it. "Some girl named Porsche sent me all your letters you sent her. She said yall was together!"

My mouth fell open. This wasn't how I wanted to tell her. I let her scream and cry it all out. When the call was cut off I called her back so she could get the rest out. I apologized and told her everything. I took full responsebility for my actions. When she hung up, I gave her time, I communicated only through letters.

After a while, I explained why I slept with all those women. We eventually started talking again. For the first time in my whole bid. I didn't get into another relationship. I did, however, start talking to this bad shorty named Domonique. I told her what I told the other girls,

"I gotta girl at home and I'm not leaving her."

She was cool with that because she had a man at home. So, we just messed around.

Time must have been high because. Next thing I knew it was two days before my release date. I finished my last pre-release physical and program. I went to the afternoon yard to kick it. I got word that this new girl was snitching. I knew the new girl from the county.

I saw her and started a conversation. We walked and talked, when we got far enough away from the Cos I punched her in her face. She fell to the ground. I had never lifted someone off their feet before. I almost hesitated in shock. One punch wasn't enough though the message had to be delivered. I jumped on top of her and started giving her head shots. I got mad because she wouldn't fight back.

I heard a CO behind say,

"Stop fighting."

I got up off of her, they cuffed me and took me to medical. By this time, I knew the drill. Sargent Smith came and asked me why we fought. I let them know we had beef from the county. He then got on the phone with the Captain on duty. After his report to the Cap. He said,

"Bailey beat the hell out that girl and played fish."

I low key laughed at the way he said that. He walked back over to me and said,

"You already know you PHC'd, go get some sleep for your release tomorrow. But Bailey, if you come back here, I promise you I'm sending you straight to S.H.U. STRAIGHT TO S.H.U."

I laughed but I knew he was serious. I told him I got him, and I didn't plan on letting him down.

# Chapter 34

ALLEY CATS

The next day I started to pack up my things that I was taking with me. I gave away a lot. It was my last night in prison. I could barely sleep. As I laid in bed reflecting on the last two years. It was a true roller coaster. There were so many moments that were literally designed to break me. There were many people who wanted to see me destroyed, reduced down to nothing.

I laid there astonished that I even made it through. I picked up my note pad and began to write,

<u>"The Journey's End</u>
One way in
How it all begins
Lawlessness
Lost souls looking for their place

Misguided coping skills
Addicted to the risk they take
Mistakes
Straighten up soldier
Hop back in that saddle
A foot on our neck
Not a stranger to this battle…see
We embrace the journey
Valiant soldiers striving for a win
Because we know that the blessings come
at the journey's end"

I laid my pen down. Took a deep breath and drifted off to sleep.

When I woke up the next morning I was ready to go. I said goodbye to all my people on my way to the reception building. I turned in my state property, I put on my parole clothes, and right as I was being processed out, I saw Dep. Johnson. "Bailey, you know you did some hard time right? Don't bring yo behind back up in here."

I laughed and told her I wasn't coming back.

I was escorted to the van for transport. I was headed to the train station. I didn't look back when we drove away from the gate. Halfway to the train station I couldn't help but give God praise. At some point the Cos joined in too. Next thing you know we were all praising Him. They gave me my train ticket and the remaining balance of my account and waved goodbye as they drove away.

As I sat on the train, my mind was blown at how much had changed in the last two years. I genuinely didn't think much would change while I was there because I only had a short time. Boy was I wrong. We had a new president, there was an app that delivered food to you now, there was even an app that you could ride share with now. what the hell was a ride share? To top it all off I missed so many good movies and musicals.

It all started to feel overwhelming. I almost started to think about the routine back in prison, before I shook that off. *I only did short time, there's no way I'm institutionalized that quick."*

I made it to the shelter. I was so grateful to see a place I was familiar with. It was starting to seem like the world was too big for me. I felt better being around some people that I knew. The staff made me feel welcome. The prison social worker had called ahead and secured a bed for me.

Since they knew where I came from, they were patient with me. They reminded me that I didn't have to ask to use the bathroom and shower. When sleeping in a room with other people around triggered me, they allowed me to sit in the dining room and talked with me. The free world was every bit of an adjustment.

My parole officer showed up at the shelter to meet me, do a drug test, and give me further instructions. My parole transfer had been approved a month before I was released. I just had to wait to get my transfer papers so I could leave. In true parole fashion it took another month to get those papers.

Granny Odessa booked my flight, and I was on my way back home to Chicago. After I landed, I was paroled to Granny Odessa house. When I got there I was put on house arrest until I saw my parole officer.

Ever since I was released, I had been in contact with Michelle. We talked every day. For the first time in two years, we didn't have to limit our conversations to 30 minutes. We took full advantage of that. It took her a while to really forgive me, but once I told her why and explained my mentality at the time we had a better understanding. I didn't tell her I was back yet; I wanted to surprise her.

I had it set up so that she came to the house to drop something off for me and I just popped out the house on her. As soon as we locked eyes it was like the first time we met for our first date. I was in love all over again. In that moment I promised to never cheat on her again. We laughed and talked like nothing had happened. Within a week we decided I would move into her apartment in Hyde Park. So, I transferred my parole to her house, and we began our lives together.

# Chapter 35

## BAD COMPANY, GOOD CHARACTER

Our first month living together was every bit of a honeymoon. It was nothing but love, joy, and nonstop smoking. We enjoyed each other's company in more ways than a few. I got her a kitten from one of my classmates. We named him *Night*. He became our little son. We were like a little family.

After a month of re-acclimation. I felt it was time for me to get into the workforce. I applied for over 20 jobs. I had at least ten interviews. At each interview I was hired on spot. Only problem was by the time my background check came back, they would call me and say,

"Unfortunately, due to your background check we are unable to extend an offer of employment at this time."

With every No I felt more and more defeated. I couldn't

catch a break. I just wanted to work. Depression started to take a toll on me. I felt hopeless. What was the point of trying if all they choose to see is the last two years of my life. I didn't apply for jobs I didn't qualify for.

When Michelle saw that I was down she jumped into action reminding me that I am worthy of a job. That made me feel better. I noticed that our bond got stronger in moments of trauma. It made me fall deeper and deeper in love with her.

One day, my cousin Bianca from my father's side called me. She said that she was stranded and needed a place to stay. I immediately jumped into action. I knew what it felt like to be homeless. And I didn't want my cousin to go through that.

I thought back to the time she saved my life on one of our family vacations. I got too bold in my swimming abilities. I jumped in the deep end and instantly started to drown. Bianca swam out, put me on her shoulders and got me back to the shallow end. The entire time she was helping me, she was underwater.

She saved my life. I wouldn't be here if it wasn't for her. The least that I could do was give her a place to sleep. I talked to Michelle about it and she agreed. We picked her up from the bus and went back to the apartment to get settled in.

It felt good to have my cousin there with me. Grandma Shirley always taught us to listen to Bianca because she was older. I looked up to her and I loved her very much. I gave her the love and respect that you would give a big sister. I would talk to her about memories from our childhood. She didn't remember any of it.

I understood though, she had been though a lot. I even overlooked the jealous face she made when I upgraded my phone. I thought maybe I just needed to show her that I'm not a person that brags or boasts. Maybe if I just show her how much I genuinely love her then maybe I could stop getting this feeling that she is envious of me.

I was so caught up in that, I was beginning to overlook Michelle. She was struggling with bills. My food stamps kept us stocked with food, but bills plus cat supplies were really starting to add up. I got back to my job search to no avail. I kept getting hired at the interview and fired later due to my background. Michelle was going to school and working. She was becoming more and more stressed by the day. I had to do something about this.

Michelle came home one Saturday crying

"what's wrong Queen?"

She replied,

"I got fired today."

I wiped her tears, ran her a bath, rolled her two blunts for herself and told her it would be alright. When she got out of the tub, I met her with the dinner I prepared.

When she fell asleep, I went into the living room and sank into the couch. I felt horrible. I had been trying and trying to get a job, but nothing has come through for me.

"What's wrong cuz?"

Bianca asked,

"Michelle got fired today and no one is trying to hire a felon."

I replied,

"Don't trip cuz, I know somebody that can help. How long have you had your bank account?"

I told her that I have had it for over 10 years.

"I know somebody who has been waiting on you. They do this all the time. You gone need to hustle to take care of home. The same way you hustled to get that phone."

No matter how much I hated to admit it, she was right.

# Chapter 36

## SMOOTH...TOO SMOOTH

The next day I got a call from an unknown number. The mane on the other line said his name so fast I didn't make out what he said. He told me he could get me some money; I said OK. We planned to meet. Bianca never told me what to expect and I didn't want to be the one to ask too many questions.

I just knew I needed to pay some bills and get an engagement ring. I had decided I wanted to marry Michelle. Since I kept getting denied by jobs I needed this money.

On the day we planned to meet my spirit felt off. I brushed it off as nerves. I was woke extra early, I decided to go get some more weed because I smoked the last of it trying to calm my nerves down. So, around about 9:30am I ran to the bank to take the last of my money out to go get a bag. When I finished my transaction, I noticed a police car pull up on me two officers got out and walked towards me. The bus pulled up just before they got to me. I hopped on the bus with a quickness and headed back to the apartment. *Why is 12 pulling up on me? And why does it feel like they knew what was going down today? The only people that knew was Bianca and ole dude. I haven't even told Michelle yet.*

I brushed it off quickly. *I'm just being paranoid. I have never done anything like this before. Nobody told me what I was getting myself into. It's just paranoia, I trust Bianca. She wouldn't do me dirty. We are family.*

I smoked a few blunts to clear my head. I just kept thinking about the money.

When it was time to link up with ole dude. I met him at the meeting spot. I got in his car, and he pulled off. I tried to get some pointers from my cousin before we left but she was nowhere to be found and wasn't answering her phone. *Why would you leave me with some random dude you put me on with. You know I don't know him nor do I know anything about his business.* I felt like I was walking blind, but I had to do this. What else was I gone do, keep getting hired and fired?

We parked close to the bank. Dude told me,
"Let me get yo card and yo pin. I'm going to go in and do it to protect you, so you not involved ok."

I said ok. I thought it was nice that he was looking out for me. I gave him what he asked for.

Another dude pulled up when he got out, I thought it was strange that dude hid his face from me as he walked pass the car. They went in and came back less than five minutes later. The new dude hid his face again, but this time I got a small glimpse of his face. Still strange that he was hiding it, I just figured it was because he didn't know me, I could understand that.

Ole dude I rode with got in the car and said,

"I'm going to keep your card and pin just to ensure you not gone do me dirty. I need your bank login too."

I had no intention of doing him dirty and I understood needing the extra security. I gave him what he asked for. He dropped me back off at the spot and he pulled off.

The next couple of days were cool. I decided not to tell Michelle until I got the bread. I checked my account periodically to see if I had money in there. By the next day both of my accounts were closed pending investigation.

# Chapter 37

DEATH TELLS

When I saw that my accounts were closed, I ran in the living room and told Bianca.

"Yall made the app hot!"

I had no clue what she meant by that.

"You and him were both checking the app. Too thirsty."

How was I supposed to know. She knew I had never done this before. She then said,

"Did you at least look at the check and sign it?"

I replied,

"What check! All I did was give dude my card, pin, and login information."

After a long pause she looked at me and said,

"Oliver, you mean to tell me you didn't sign the check!?"

I had never even written a check in my life. I only ever used

debit. After I told her no, she responded,
"I didn't think I had to tell you to sign the check!"

I was forced to tell Michelle because she used my other account. Just as I was telling her what happened the bank called me concerning the check. The man on the phone sounded like he already knew what it was.
"Where did you get the check?"
I was so caught off guard I stuttered slightly when I told him I lost my wallet on the bus. Then I hung up.
Bianca said,
"You gone have to go into the bank because look at how you are sounding. Go get your girl money. Tell them you lost your wallet on the bus."
When I got to the bank I tried to take her money out my other account but they said I couldn't. A banker walked up to me and invited me to a cubicle and said,
"Your accounts were flagged for fraud. Do you know anything about this."
I said exactly what I was told to say.
"I lost my wallet when I got on the bus."
The banker wrote down what I said.
When I got back to the apartment ole dude that picked me up called me and said,

"I heard you went to the bank. You know that could be dangerous for me."
I told him what I said. He sounded skeptical. His tone indicated that he thought that I was some snitch. He continued,
"I had somebody snitch on me before and I'm not trying to go through that again."

I told him,

"I ain't no snitch"

Then he hung up. I immediately called Bianca.

"That dude you connected me with, called me about going into the bank. I told him what I said. I said exactly what you told me to say. Then he hung up. I think dude thinks I snitched can you talk-"

Before I could get the rest out Bianca interrupts me and says,

"What!"

Then she hung up the phone. She didn't answer the next five times I called back. When she finally answered,

"I was trying to ask you to talk to him before you hung up on me. Dude didn't out right say I snitched. His tone implied that was what he was thinking. Maybe I heard him wrong."

She began to yell at me,

"What you mean! You just got that boy killed!"

Then she hung up.

# Chapter 38

## WRONG UNDERSTANDING

"You just got that boy killed!"

It was like the words were constantly repeating, tormenting me with every replay.

"How could I be responsible for that? I never said who I was even talking about. I never gave her a name."

I didn't tell her to kill anyone. I got the word talk out before she hung up. I literally wanted to grab air and put it into my lungs because they were not working. I was being blamed for a body that I never requested.

In my panic, I broke down every word of our conversation. Nowhere in our conversation did I ask for or even felt like someone should die. I believed that my cousin would talk to the guy that picked me up. I believed that after the talk we would move pass this. If I thought that conversation would lead to someone's death I wouldn't have called her in the first place.

I have never been the one to have someone fight my battles. I fight my own battles. I know she heard me say talk. I began to second guess myself. *Did I say it quick enough? Am I really to blame? That's not the person I am!*

Way too many thoughts ran through my mind. I knew exactly what I needed to do. I was alone in the apartment. I laid face down on the floor. And I prayed,

"Heavenly Father I repent. I repent for not waiting on you and leaning to my own understanding. I confess with my mouth that I went off your path you had for me God. I need you Abba, please don't leave me I repent. Please help me. I am being blamed for something I didn't do. Abba, you know my heart and intentions. You know that I asked her to talk to him. God, you know the type of person I am. I confessed with my mouth that I have sinned against you. I tried to get money deceitfully and I lied to that banker. I ran right off the path you have for me. I surrender to you Abba. Not my will but your will be done in my life. I pray this prayer in the name of the Father, the Son, and the Holy Spirit."

I laid on the floor and sobbed for a while. I released everything that I wanted to happen concerning my life. I accepted that I was giving God permission to take the wheel in my life. I didn't care about how I looked. I didn't care that so many people told me that God wouldn't love me because of my lifestyle. I fully surrendered to Him. I left it all on that floor.

When I got off that floor, I remembered what Pawpaw used to say every time I cried as a kid.

"Stop crying baby, go wash your face."

When Michelle got home, I told her what happened. I let her

know that I couldn't take the rest of her check out. I can't say I blamed her for being mad at me.

Bianca got back to the apartment later that night. She acted like nothing happened.  She seemed happy like she just got some good news.

"Hey cuz guess what. I found out about this place hiring. You should check it out. I heard they are having a hiring event today."

I didn't have time even to address her nonchalant behavior. I rushed to put on my interview clothes and ran out the door to the interview with a couple copies of my resume in hand.

I got off the bus just in time. Everyone was lined up outside the door. I got in line just as they let everyone in. I had a great interview. Afterwards the interviewer informed me that they wanted to hire me. I filled out all the necessary paperwork and got the information for orientation.

I was so excited about getting a job I almost didn't notice the dude I had never seen at the apartment before standing at the entrance text someone as I came pass and before he walked off…. Almost.

"They're watching me."

I thought to myself as I got into the apartment. I was now back in survival mode.

Michelle was very happy that I had the job.

"See baby I told you eventually you would get one."

With my first check I paid her back the money she lost on top of what I was able to pay towards the bills. I was so happy to be working again.  I couldn't help but thank God for this blessing. I worked hard. Even my parole officer said I was at work more than I was at home.

I came home one day, and Michelle told me that Bianca had

to go. She said what happened with that situation didn't sit well with her. She let me know she wasn't comfortable with her being there anymore. I was torn because I still loved my cousin, but Something just didn't feel right concerning her.

# Chapter 39

## THE SWITCH

I was straightening up after Bianca left, I saw a bird's feather under the chest she slept next to. I don't know how that bird feather got there. I felt a feeling in my stomach urging me not to touch it, but I brushed it off. I picked it up and threw it away.

Over the next few weeks, I noticed me and Michelle arguing more. She felt distant. We were doing fine before Bianca left so I was a little lost as to why. I noticed that Michelle and one of her friends giving off signs that they were former sex partners. Now as a person who was locked up before I know exactly what it looked like to be with somebody and pretend like you're not with them. In prison if they knew you were a couple, they would separate you.

I decided to ask Michelle about it. I let her know if they did have sex in the past, I wouldn't be mad. I would understand. I had my fair share of fun in prison so I wouldn't even trip about it. She informed me that she had never had sex with her friend I said ok and I moved on.

It wasn't until I was at work and her friend came into my job to buy something and caught up with me on her way out and said,

"Hey big homie, I just left yo crib dropping off a bag. Your girl got it smelling like some good steak and potatoes up in there."

I laughed and thanked her for dropping off a bag. I caught the sneaky undertone in her voice. I kept cool. I learned a lot from Honey and her lies. I would never let a mug see me sweat. So when I got home I tested what she said,

"Hey Baby, did your friend drop off the bag. I got blunts."
She replied,

"Yea baby."
I then asked her,

"Did she come upstairs or did you go downstairs."
She said as smooth as butter,

"I went downstairs baby."
I still didn't want to jump to conclusions, so I went to the kitchen where she was cooking dinner. I looked in the skillet and saw a steak.

"I fixed your favorite tonight baby."
Then she kissed me and went to make a plate. I instantly lost my appetite. I tried to brush it off. I thought maybe she smelled it on her clothes. I just couldn't bring myself to believe that she would play me like that.

I still couldn't get it out of my head when I asked her if they ever hooked up. She said no. I told her I wouldn't get mad if they did. Why would she lie? I started to have dreams about them sleeping together. I decided to dive into work to clear my head.

I remember my mama saying,

"To be aware is to be alive."

That stuck with me.

One day my coworker asked me to switch shifts. So, on the day they worked my shift I had to pick up a few things for dinner. I pulled up and I heard Holy Spirit say,

"Stay in the car."

I sat for a little while with the car running. I saw this dude come out of my job with a mask on he had his left hand on a handgun that was tucked in his too tight ripped jeans. We locked eyes and I slowly put the car in drive. *I may get shot, but you not gone live to celebrate.*

It was all that went through my head. I heard Holy Spirit again,

"Hold."

My eyes never left him. I watched as he got in his car and pulled off. I thanked God for his grace and mercy. I thanked him also for sending the Holy Spirit to help me in that moment. I walked into the store, got my items and went home.

# Chapter 40

## CATCH A BREAK

Me and Michelle started to drift apart. The dreams of her cheating kept coming. Every time we hung out with her friends, I always had the feeling they knew something I didn't. I saw more and more red flags constantly.

One day Michelle was late getting home from school. I called her and she said she was with ole girl. We usually plan when we re-up. This time she didn't tell me she was going over there. I asked her if she was coming home soon and she said,
"Yea I had to leave school early because it was a long drive to get to her."

I tried my best not to say anything. I heard how she seductively said her. She said her like she just got her back blown out. I chuckled and said,

"Iigh Queen I'll see you when you get home."

It took her an hour to drive the 15-minute drive home. When she came in, we argued. She gas lit me every time I brought up a concern. She said I was just being paranoid and insecure. Needless to say, I slept on the couch that night.

After I got off the next day she apologized and gave some lame excuse as to why she was late. I knew she was lying. I thought about all I had done in prison; I decided to let it slide. I said if she was really sorry, she would stop talking to her and get a new connect. She agreed and we moved forward.

A week later I picked up her phone because it rang while she was in the shower. I saw text messages between her and ole girl. We argued about it and I told her to choose. Her or me? She responded by saying,

"I shouldn't have to stop talking to someone. Just because you're insecure."

I packed a bag and had her drop me off at my granny Odessa house. I needed a break.

Unfortunately, a break was out of reach for me. I had no peace at home and no peace at the job that used to be my outlet. I had more and more people coming in to watch me. I had a new manager micromanaging me. It was becoming overwhelming. I had to endure it though. This was my only form of income. I just continued to pray every day. I remembered a scripture saying to pray without ceasing. That's exactly what I planned to do.

Me and Michelle eventually made up. I moved back in with her. Things were going pretty good. I started a job search after I had a dream that I got hired at another job. My cousin posted on her social media that her job was hiring. Me and Michelle both applied. We both got hired.

I praised God for showing up and showing out in my life. I knew that I was unworthy, but God never stopped loving me. Even when I turned my back on Him. Shortly after being hired, I had my last Parole Visit. I couldn't believe two years had passed. I was now officially free from the judicial system. It had been a long four years. So much had happened.

I didn't even feel like the same person. I had a higher paying job. Weed was now legal. The new job didn't even care about my background. I finally felt like I was actually about to catch a break.

# *Chapter 41*

## BIGGER PICTURE

**M**y new manager Amy is amazing. She is a great leader. I can tell that she really loves what she is doing. The activities she organized were activities that our residents truly enjoyed.

One Monday, we got the news that a sickness was going around. More and more of our residents were getting sick. It was now mandatory for all employees to receive a vaccine to work. We had to go through extensive training, we canceled all group activities. I had a couple suggestions on how to keep morale up. My suggestions were heard and became successful.

Eventually they made one floor the quarantine floor. They needed someone to provide activities for the Residents on that floor. I volunteered to take it. Apart of me was nervous about it, from what we were told about this sickness, we knew this virus was highly contagious. I promptly put this to the back of my mind.

I was determined to take their minds off all the emotions that came with that sickness. The fear we all felt at this time could be overwhelming. I was determined to do my part and bring as much joy as I possibly could. For some Residents this was the scariest time of their lives.

The hardest part was watching Residents that I had created bonds with go from being perfectly healthy, smiling, and full of life; to being frail, scared, and dying. Residents that I shared so many laughs with. People like Paul whose life stories and kind nature were so refreshing while we smoked our squares. We always seemed to run into each other when I went out for my break. Jim, who smiled nonstop, every time I came to drop off activities for him. Sometimes we would just sit and talk. He was only in for rehabilitation from an amputated leg. He was about to be released.

We lost over 50 residents, the world was on lock down, and every day we came in to work to find out that another one of our residents was dead. Good people…dead. People we made laugh…dead. people who made us feel joy while we tried to make them happy…dead. Many of our co-workers died as well. There was so much death around us.

I couldn't dwell on it. There was still an assignment. I couldn't think about it. I had to stay focused.

Apparently, Michelle felt the same way. She decided to distract herself by cozying up to the girl that was doing valet. I came outside so we could go to lunch together and she was in the valet girl's car.
"You must think I'm a fucking goofy. Get the fuck out this car. So we can go eat."

She tried to explain but I wasn't trying to hear it. We went to get lunch in silence. It took everything in me not to put hands and feet on the valet girl as we walked back in to work. I refused to give her satisfaction. My patience was wearing thin with Michelle. I know I messed up in prison, but I have changed.

I quickly pushed that out of my mind. Keeping our resident's morale high had to be the focal point.

*They were the bigger picture.*

# Chapter 42

## WAY TOO MUCH

It took a long time for me to stop feeling like I was walking into a tomb at work. Even though the deaths slowed down, and the world came off lock down, the feeling didn't go away. So many things had changed in the world. Masks were now a part of our lives, social distancing was the new norm, and many people lost their jobs and livelihoods.

Me and Michelle decided it was time for a vacation. We realized that we had been in survival mode so long we hadn't even had a chance to mourn the people we lost at work. We got invited to go to Las Vegas by my bro Terrell. So, we took our PTO and decided we were headed to Las Vegas. Our bro Tony also joined us. We were so hyped. To just have a moment to get away and relax.

As soon as we got there, we looked for a dispensary. We got

our supplies. We smoked then headed back to our room to decide what we wanted to do later that night. We decided to walk the strip for a while. After walking along the strip, we decided to go get some dinner.

While we were heading to a restaurant for dinner, I noticed Terrell and Michelle sharing private jokes. As we were walking he made sure to walk close to her as they shared hushed conversations and laughter. I thought that was weird because Terrell brought a female he was talking to with him, but he was walking and talking with Michelle more.

I kept my cool. I wanted to watch before I jumped to conclusions. At dinner Terrell sat between Michelle and his shorty. Most of his conversations were towards Michelle. He was barely talking to the bros. it felt like we were guest in their conversation.

I'm trying my best not to make a face, but I couldn't help the side eye. This whole scene was giving side chick vibes. *I know she didn't sleep with the bro!*

When we got back to the room I asked her about it. I low key wouldn't have been mad. Again, I was away for two years. I just wanted her to keep it real with me. She told me I was tripping, and she would never do that to me.

I had a dream that night of her cheating on me with Terrell. The next morning, I couldn't get the dream out of my head. I tried to play it cool but whole time I wanted to spazz out. Tony pulled me to the side. I was able to get some stuff off my chest during our bro talk. I felt a lot better and chose just to enjoy the rest of our trip.

When we got back home, we had a day of rest, then it was back to work. I had a new manager named Mary. She was nice but it always seemed like she was, too nice. It felt like she was doing too much. She began to micro-manage me. She was always looking over my shoulder. I noticed that her focus was only on me. She assured me it wasn't personal, but it felt very personal.

She started to remove me from activities that I had been doing long before she was hired. She shot down every new suggestion I had. Her activity ideas were mediocre to say the least. The nice facade turned to passive aggression quickly. She always followed her passive aggressive behavior with food for us. I caught on to her tactics and stopped eating what she ordered. One day she randomly asked me if I wanted some water. She said she was going to get some for herself and wanted to know if I wanted some. I noticed she didn't ask my coworker in the room with us if she wanted some water. Then when I declined the water she never went to go get the cup of water that she said she was going to get to myself.

During a staff meeting she said that she wanted to dismantle the activities cart, were our residents would do activities and earn tickets to buy items off the cart. I explained how much our residents loved the cart and dismantling it without a better replacement could cause a lot of our residents to loose their sense of purpose. My co-workers agreed with me and we all opposed the dismantling of the activities cart. She then asked everyone to leave so she could take to me privately. I explained as professionally as I could that I was not interested in a private conversation. I began to walk out of the office and she proceeded to follow me into the hallway saying,

"I want to talk to you."

She followed me all the way to the elevators, I began to feel harassed. I turned around and started to walk towards HR's office. I explained everything that was going on and she dismissed me. Mary tried to follow me out of the office. Just as she was about to walk out after me HR stopped her. I was so grateful for that because Mary was doing way too much.

## *Chapter 43*

## HIDDEN ACTIVITIES

A few minutes after their conversation, Mary came and apologized to me. I forgave her and hoped that things would change. Of course, things didn't change, she was right back to her same behavior the next day. Enough was enough. I expressed my concerns to the director, and she called her director so that we could all have a meeting. When they sided with Mary I handed in my letter of resignation.

I started putting in applications a week prior to this meeting. I had an interview scheduled for later that week. I was starting to understand God's timing more. I felt that it was time to leave that job. I also knew that I had to go by God's timing.

Later that week I had my interview. I was hired on the spot to work with youth in the foster system. I was scheduled to start the following week. I met the young guys I was going to

158

be working with. The first week went well. Around the third week I started to notice a lot of staring from the older kids and their staff. It looked like they were gearing up for war. People kept asking me where I lived and if I had family nearby. The questions became more and more personal. At one point I was talking to another staff member and about 6 of the older boys ran up to me like they wanted to fight me. This big 350-pound six-foot three staff member named Maurice said,

"Not Yet."

They all stopped. I asked God silently,

"Heavenly Father why did you send me here?"

I heard a still, quiet voice say,

"To pray over this land and call upon my name here."

I wasted no time doing exactly what God said. I prayed silently over the land and each child that lived there. I was still having a conversation with my coworker when God began to reveal some things to me. He revealed that someone was planning for my death. The revelation was so powerful I spoke it out loud. My coworker looked at me like I was crazy.

I started to notice people putting poles, broom sticks, bricks, and big rocks around the group home. I felt in my spirit that it was time to go. I grabbed my stuff, and I walked out. I called my mama on the way. I remembered mama had street knowledge and I figured she would know what to do. I asked her how to handle it. She told me to call my boss and tell them what was going on. She was more concerned about me loosing my job. I understood where she was coming from, but I wasn't gone be a snitch for no one.

I called my boss and simply requested not to work in that building anymore, Saying that I was switched to that building last minute and it wasn't my assigned building, I requested to stay in my assigned building. My boss immediately starts laughing. She asked why and I told her I didn't want to discuss why. I told her I would like to stay in my assigned house. She told me to call this higher up named Jose'. I called him and restated my request and when he asked why I said the same thing that I told my boss. Apparently, that wasn't good enough for him because he kept asking the same question in different ways. *I might have to make up something so that he can finally leave me alone about it and accept my request.*

I cultivated a story. He told me I could leave, and we ended the call. I prayed and repented to God for lying. As I was walking off the property, Maurice walked up to me aggressively. I immediately took my bookbag off and prepared myself to fight. Maurice began to yell,
"What you lie for! You taking off your bookbag like you tough or something?"
I didn't say a word, I had to stay focused on his attack. This man was way bigger than me. I knew I had to give it all I had. I felt bad about the lie, but I would rather lie than snitch.

Maurice squared up with me and hit me with a left hook straight to the face. His punch felt like a feather touched my face. I barely felt that. He noticed that I ate his first punch and hesitated to punch me again. That gave me just enough time to punch him dead in his throat as hard as I could. He stumbled. Just as he was about to rush me again my coworkers stepped in and broke up the fight. I felt like I just fought Goliath.

I heard multiple footsteps running up behind me. I turned and prepared for war. One of the therapists on site had arrived and signaled to the boys to stop. They stopped in their tracks. Maurice stormed off yelling,

"The next time I see you I'm killing you!"

The staff member who heard me speak God's revelation offered to escort me off campus. As we walked, he said,

"We were just talking about this earlier."

He looked perplexed then he asked me,

"Hey, did God say anything to you about me?"

The fact that he even asked baffled me. I prayed and asked God what did want me to say. I replied,

"God said that you are a good judge of character."

One of the young kids that was with Maurice. Walked up to me to fight, but my coworker stopped him. Just as he turned him around and walked him back to the building, God gave me another revelation. The weight of it almost dropped me to my knees. Maurice was molesting that boy.

# Chapter 44

## GOT EM

I know how a child acts when they have been touched inappropriately. I prayed and asked God for confirmation. I received it in a dream, and it dawned on me. I was sent to that job for a reason. Well, it was time to look for another job…again.

During this time, me and Michelle just could not see eye to eye. Our dysfunction was becoming more and more stressful. We decided it was time to take a break. I moved back in with my granny Odessa. I thought the space would help but as soon as I walked into her house, I felt this overwhelming feeling of despair. I was upset about my breakup, but this was way more intense. I couldn't sleep, eat, or pray. Even my dreams were foggy.

I also noticed that the block was busier than it usually was.

Our block was usually quiet.  After I moved in there were always people driving down the block. There was this silver car always parked across the street from the house. Whenever I talked about it with granny Odessa, she would tell me that I'm just being paranoid.  Yet, every time we stepped outside her body language told me she knew something. I had told her everything that happened with Bianca. Yet, she was moving weirdly. She kept saying,

"That's why you have to be careful with the decisions you make."

And

"Our words are powerful; we must choose our words wisely."

One day my uncle Brandon started asking me questions he had never asked me before. Questions like,

"You out here by yourself?"

"How long you gone be out here?"

"Where are you staying?"

The biggest lesson I learned in prison was never to trust the person asking too many questions. Shoot that was the reason I didn't ask any Questions with Bianca.

I would confide in my mama, but she would tell me I was being paranoid too.  She would say that my uncle was just worried about my well-being. Yet, when we would go out she was always looking nervous like a bullet was coming through the window at any moment. I was kicking it with her one night and it got late.

"Iigh ma can I get a ride to granny house?"

She quickly said,

"Naw I need you to stay with mama tonight. I want you to sleep right here."

As she pointed to the couch. The way she said it caused all

types of red flags for me. First, she has a whole empty bedroom with a bed in it. Why does she want me on the couch cushion. I heard Holy Spirit say,

"Leave now."

I told Mama I couldn't stay.  She reluctantly agreed.  She looked scared to death on the ride to granny house.  While she was looking nervous, I had the intense feeling that my obedience to God's instruction just saved my life.

It wasn't until I laid in my bed that it hit me like a ton of bricks to the chest. My mama just tried to set me up. I cried myself to sleep that night. The next day I called Michelle, we had been talking back and forth for a while. We had decided to still be friends. We both came to realize that we still loved each other.

When Michelle didn't answer I didn't trip. I called her an hour later, still no answer. Three hours later she video calls me with every bit of sex hair. If you know, you just know. I couldn't get words to come out of my mouth. I just stared at her. We had only been broken up for a week. She automatically started to explain why she didn't answer the phone. I just stared at her. I studied her as she lied so smoothly with an slight undertone of nervousness. I hung up the phone and put it on do not disturb.

It was at this moment that I knew I was having a psychotic break. It was like everything was crashing in on me at once. I'm unemployed, People sitting outside the house watching me.  Getting evil stares everywhere I go, feeling as if a false narrative has been placed on my head, family trying to line me up, the woman I loved and was just talking about getting back together with is having sex with someone else.  Not to mention the fact that she called me baby right before I hung up the phone. It was too much. I was reaching a breaking point.

Before I knew it, I was lying on the floor in a ball sobbing. Granny Odessa stood me on my feet and started to pray. Something felt off about her prayer. It was like she wasn't praying to the God of Abraham, Issac, and Jacob. As she prayed, she began beating her fist on my chest. Every blow reminded me of when she would "discipline" me growing up. That was it. I needed help.

I ran to the bathroom locked the door and called for an ambulance. I explained to dispatch that I needed a psychological evaluation. When the paramedics arrived, Granny Odessa attempted to block the door. The police came as well, and I was able to get out of the house. She yelled from the doorway,
"You better tell them everything too!"
The officer glared at Granny Odessa then said to me,
"You don't have to tell me anything. Let's go get you some help."
When we got to the psych ward. They began their intake. I couldn't sit still. I was talking fast. Something felt completely off in my spirit. When they gave me a shot to calm me, I noticed a man wearing scrubs standing in the distance with a surgical mask on. When my eyes met his, I instantly froze. I knew those eyes. I felt a sense of dread creeping up in me. Maurice.

Just as the meds kicked in and I drifted off to sleep I heard another staff member say,
"Got yo ass."

# Chapter 45

MY SAVIOR

When I woke up a man and a woman were wheeling down this dark hallway. I heard one of them say, "We are not sending her there. She will stay right here. No one is killing anyone."

I was in and out of consciousness during the second intake. When we got to my room the man said,

"Don't worry you're safe now."

Soon as I got into bed I passed out.

I woke up groggy thinking that yesterday was a dream. I remember hearing the words, you're safe now. Those words provided some comfort. I took a shower and put the clothes they laid out for me. I felt refreshed, I looked out the window thanking God for a safe place to recharge. I heard the door open, and a dude stood in the doorway. He was a spitting image of Maurice.

He had to be Maurice's older brother.  The safe feeling I had just flew out of the window. My survival mode had been reactivated. I was in a lion's den. Granny Odessa had a saying about this.  When you got your hand in a lion's mouth you pat it on the head. She would always say. I never completely understood that growing up.  I was always one to say when your hand is in a lions mouth you rip his tongue out. I clearly wasn't the one with wisdom.

"I just came to check on you."

I thanked him for checking on me.

"You thought you were locked in here?"

I couldn't help but laugh. Informed him that I thought I had to be let out like in prison.  There was a hint of confusion in his eyes as he explained that I could leave the room at any time. He explained that the door locks every time I closed it, so that no one could come in my room unless they had a key.

They called for breakfast. When I got there, I was able to see who else was in the ward with me. I noticed two guys staring at me. One had matted hair and the other had tattoos on his face. They stared at me with evil intent in their eyes. I felt the need to avoid them. After breakfast, we had a program. Once program was done, I went to go watch T.V. as I was sitting there, I heard Holy Spirit's voice say,

"Go lock in your room, I don't want you in here."

The two guys were walking in as I was walking out. They both mugged me like they were just waiting for the signal to do something to me.  I mentally went back into jail mode. I began to feel a feeling of dread and fear, but it went away when I started to pray. I heard God say,

"You will not die here, stay in my presence. Stay in this room."

After I heard his voice, I saw a sparrow land on the window seal outside my window. I took that as confirmation. A couple hours later Maurice's brother, who I now know as Tyrone, let me know it was time to meet my psych doctor.

I sat down with Dr. Kravsky.

"Are you feeling suicidal?"

"How are you feeling today?"

"What brought you in today."

I answered his questions briefly. I informed him that I wasn't feeling suicidal, I let him know I was feeling well rested after last night, and I explained to him about being unemployed and my recent break up. He asked if I had a history of problems sleeping. I informed him that I did and in less than five minutes he diagnosed me with bipolar disorder and prescribed me sleeping medication.

When they came to give our night meds, I found out that Dr. Kravsky prescribed me a sleeping pill that my body was used to taking. After I took my meds I noticed different people were coming to do my 30 minute checks. It literally was a different person every time. Because my body was used to the meds I took, I was able to wake up every time the door opened.

I eventually drifted off to sleep. I was jolted out of my sleep. I heard Holy Spirit say,

"Wake up, go close the door."

When I got up to close the door, I noticed that the door wasn't closed all the way. About 10 minutes later I heard what appeared to be a heavy duffle bag drop to the floor outside my door. I heard the handle jiggle, but the door didn't open. I silently shouted for joy, because I knew God just saved my life.

# Chapter 46

## NO WEAPON FORMED

I could tell from the look on everybody's face the next morning, that nobody expected me to walk out of that room. I heard Holy Spirit say,

"Stay calm the rest of your time here."

They refused to give me my outside clothes like everyone else. Forcing me to stay in the hospital gown. I didn't say anything. I started cheeking my night meds and spitting them out in the toilet. I slept during the day and stayed awake at night.

I saw the doctor again a day later. I let him know I was doing fine and was ready to be released. He checked to see if I had attended all programs. He also checked to see if I had taken my meds. Although I was spitting them out later the record still showed that I took them. He checked with the staff to see if I had caused any problems. When everything checked out he said I could be released that day.

When they released me, my mama came to pick me up. She drove up looking scared. She pulled my niece out of the car and almost threw her into my arms. Whole time she was looking at the dude who escorted me out. It felt as if she was low key saying,

"I got a baby with me don't shoot."

I rode silently in the car. I didn't know who to trust. I just survived an attack on my life just to get released into a war zone. *Out of the frying pan into the fire.*

The next week flew by. I applied for a new job directing the activities department at an assisted living community. I had my interview and got hired on the spot. I was now making more money than I had ever made in my life. Me and Michelle decided to get back together. We moved back in with each other. Besides the usual stalkers following me around everywhere, things were going well.

I was getting positive feedback from my new job. Our community was even getting recognition from the higher ups. I was learning so much and having a lot of fun with our residents. God was really doing His big one. It felt like a complete turnaround. I was so happy I almost didn't notice the hushed conversations going on around me.

Our HR rep Mrs. Jones, who seemed excited to hire me, suddenly started to act like she hated me, and I didn't understand why. I had never been anything but kind to her. I treated her with nothing but respect. Yet, she started to act like she wanted to taste my blood and dance on my grave.

One day I was scrolling on social media. Her profile popped up as someone I may know. I figured it was because we had a lot of friends in common. I clicked on her profile out of pure curiosity. As I scrolled down her page, I almost dropped my phone when I saw a picture of the guy that met Ole Dude and me at the bank. He was the guy that hid his face. In the caption it read

"R.I.P. SON"

I wondered if she thought I killed her son. I hadn't even said two words to him. He wasn't even the guy that called me that day. *Am I being blamed for something?* I had nothing to do with this man's death. I felt sick to my stomach, but it was all coming together. Now I understand why I was being talked about more and more at the job. All the evil stares. People were looking at me like they had me cornered. This was getting to be toxic quickly.

One day I got into a ride share on my way home. When we got close to the apartment, I saw the driver text someone saying they were 11 minutes away. I looked at the map and it said exactly 11 minutes away. We stopped at a red light next to a gas station. I looked out the window and I saw Maurice sitting at a gas pump. We locked eyes and I calmly texted my family that lived close and positioned myself defensively. I remembered what Pawpaw used to say, *Never let them take you to the second location.*

I was ready for war. We pulled up to the apartment I stood outside for a little bit to see if he had tailed us. I was ready for whatever. I thanked God as I walked into the apartment. This was the second time I had seen Maurice, after his death threat, and survived. God is good.

Michelle was away on a girls trip. When she returned, I told her what had happened, and she told me I was just being paranoid. Two weeks later she got into a bad accident. She said it sounded like they sped up. When I heard that I knew what it was, it was an attempt on her life. She survived. I thanked God. She only had some scrapes and bruises. The next week we both went to the dealership and got two new cars. The weapon formed, but didn't prosper.

<h1 style="text-align:center">Chapter 47</h1>

## DIVINE DETOUR

When Michelle was all healed up she went on another girls trip to New Orleans. She came back saying she wanted to live there. We both agreed it would be a great move for her. Two weeks later she moved down there and stayed with her cousin until she got an apartment.

A month and a half later she had an apartment, and I started to look for jobs down there as well. I got a job as a group home manager serving neurodivergent adults. I was taking a major pay cut but I loved this field. I remember when I was supposed to be trained to be a supervisor before I went to prison. I felt that this was the opportunity to redeem myself.

Michelle's mom decided to move in with us as well. I had always loved Michelle's mom. I considered us to be a little family. I was excited to live with her. Everything started off cool. I loved the new job and home life was good as well.

About five months in Me and Michelle were back arguing again. And her mother was now causing arguments. Me and Michelle broke up and I homeless in another state yet again.

Outside of my personal life being in shambles, I was doing a great job being a home manager. The group home I worked at did a complete turnaround since I started. The guys that I served were doing better than ever. They were learning new skills. Holy Spirit told me that I had to prepare the table for the next. I had no idea what that meant but I was determined to be obedient.

One day Holy Spirit told me it was time to go to my next assignment. I asked God where he was taking me. And Holy Spirit said…Oklahoma.

"Oklahoma!?"

I packed up my car, checked out of the hotel I was living out of and drove to Oklahoma the next day. For the next three months I bounced around from hotel to hotel. Many changes happened during this time.

At the first hotel I quit smoking weed and squares. At the second hotel I quit drinking. The third hotel I denounced my homosexuality, joined a church, and got baptized. At the fourth hotel I cut my beard off and realized that being transgender was an idol for me. I decided to DE-transition. When I got to the fifth hotel, I changed my wardrobe and heard Holy Spirit call me to publish a book of my poetry.

I finally humbled myself and became obedient to God's will and began collecting my poetry and writing new poems. While I was in prayer one day I heard Holy Spirit say,

"It is time for your next assignment."

I asked God where he was sending me. His reply was,

"Malta"

I remembered the story of the Apostle Paul getting bit by a snake in Malta. I asked God why he wants me to go there. He replied,

"To get bit by a snake, but fear not. You must get bit to make it to your next."

I surrendered to God's will, packed up my things, and headed to my Malta. *Chicago*

When I got there, I linked up with my cousin Tyra. She said she would call around and see if anyone was renting a room.

One of her guy friends contacted her saying he was renting a room. We rushed over and took a tour of the house. After touring the room and house everything seemed to be in order. Granny Odessa sent the money needed to secure the room and I went to the store to buy some stuff for the room.

When I got everything in the room, I heard God say,

"My child you have just been bit."

I didn't understand what he meant by that until about three days later. I noticed this older lady sitting outside my door. She sat there literally all day. It was as if she was placed there to watch my going and coming. I couldn't go to the bathroom without her watching me.

When I got there, I was fasting. one night in prayer God gave me the most detailed instructions to date. He said,

"Extend your fast, there is a camera in your room the blind spot is in the closet. Take your bookbag with you every time you leave. Fill the bag with your essentials. When you get somewhere safe dump your essentials in your trunk. Take only what you can fit in your bookbag. Don't use the bathroom at night. Stop all liquids two hours before bed. When you are here stay in your room. Don't stop writing. In three days you will leave this place and go where I will send you."

I almost felt overwhelmed by God's instructions, but I trusted Him, and I was determined to be obedient to His word. That night I heard people shuffling outside my bedroom door. I thanked God for His instructions that very moment.

When I woke up the next morning, I continued to pack my bookbag. I dumped the items in my trunk as instructed by God. When I got back, they were serving dinner and I heard the house manager say,

"Hey, take this plate upstairs to Maurice."

I thanked God again because now it all made sense. I had a revelation. *Our obedience is not based on whether we understand God's plan, Or not. Even if we don't understand what God is doing, obedience is to submit knowing that God's will is best.*

I locked myself in the room for the rest of the night and prepared for church the next day. When I woke up, I showered and got dressed. On my way out of the door I heard God say,

"This is your deliverance."

I knew I wasn't coming back after church. When the church let out, I got in the car and drove to Springfield IL. I put applications all over and a job in Springfield was the only one who contacted me back. I got a bed at the shelter there. It was a 30 day emergency housing situation.

The job that contacted me scheduled an interview. I attended the interview and had a great interview in my opinion. I was hired then they ran a background check. I had hoped my background would be ignored due to my many years of experience in the field. Unfortunately, they retracted their offer when the results came back.

When my move out date came at the shelter, the manager

refused to extend my housing like she did for the other women. I was forced to sleep in my car. When I called Granny Odessa, she said I could come stay with her. She had recently moved to Alabama. The whole way done there I asked God why He sent me there. His response was,

"You had to take the detour to get to your next."

# Chapter 48

YOUR TIME HERE HAS EXPIRED

I made it to Birmingham in record time. Granny Odessa welcomed me with open arms. While she hugged me, I heard God say,

"I'm about to make your enemies bless you."

At this point I stopped trying to prematurely understand what God says to me. At this point I knew to just wait and see.

I truly enjoyed spending time with granny. She would go out of her way to tell me that I was safe. She said that a lot. It felt good to just be able to take a breath. I kept writing my poetry. In the back of my mind, I was wondering who was going to start blessing me. So, I would know who my enemy was. Just as I thought that my granny asked if I wanted to go shopping. I froze before answering. *It couldn't be. She raised me?!*

I thought if I helped more around the house she would

change her mind.  She has always claimed to be a child of God. She goes to church every Sunday. It couldn't be her.

One morning I was up early reading the bible when I overheard her bible study conversation.  I was expecting to hear discussions about scriptures and prayers, but all I heard was her gossiping about somebody. I felt the veil starting to come off.

I didn't want to believe it. I saw her starting to get annoyed with me helping around the house. When I cooked, she would constantly stand over me after I let her know repeatedly, I didn't like that.  It was as if she cared nothing about my boundaries.  She went out of her way to purposefully step on every boundary I set.

I decided to go to church with her. The church was on this back road back up in the woods. The first red flag, they had foil in all the windows. *Y'all already back up in the woods. What's the foil for?"*

Second red flag, there was only 10 people in the church. And 6 of them were related to the pastor. There were spider webs everywhere. As a certified church baby, I knew something was not right in this church.

Something felt off about the pastor's husband, it felt like he had a relationship going on with his young granddaughter. She couldn't be more than 10 years old, but her body language said she was his woman. The pastor's daughter was giving an I'm nice but I'm not that nice vibe.

At the end of the service, the pastor grabbed this bottle of oil and began 'anointing' everyone. When it came to me, she touched my stomach. I found that weird. I noticed right after that, I didn't get my period that month. That was the last day I went to that church.

After that Granny started to act weird too. One day she made a pot of chit'lins, when she was done she portioned them in Ziplock bags. She never did that before, usually she would let everybody know the food was ready then put away the leftovers. She put her and grandpa's name on their bag and put a Ziplock bag in the drawer were I put my stuff. She also put a bag in the freezer. When I looked at that bag I heard God say, "Don't eat that."

I obeyed and about a week went by and she asked me why I hadn't eaten the food yet. I told her I wasn't in the mood for it and I thanked her for putting some aside for me. She became furious and grabbed the bag out of the drawer and threw it in the garbage.

I wondered why she got so mad and threw the food away. A couple days later I asked her why she threw the food away. She told me she never threw them away as she showed me the bag in the freezer. I noticed she was lying a lot lately.

One day I wanted to talk about some things that happened when I was growing up. As I read my bible more me and God began a healing journey. I wanted to have a heartfelt conversation. I also hoped that if we strengthened our bond then she wouldn't want to be my enemy anymore.

When I brought them up, she denied even doing these things and called me a liar. She lied multiple times about trivial things. I just could not understand her lies. She was always the one saying how she hated a liar, but she is constantly lying.

My little cousin came to visit. At first we were having a wonderful time. I noticed that her annoyance with my presence began to rise. I was starting to feel like she didn't want me there. Her conversation with me became more and more provoking.

It was like she was trying to get a reaction out of me. I saw the bait and I refused to take it. That made her angrier.

One night she got mad because I didn't put the top on a plate that I warmed up in the microwave. I got up to put the top on it. She didn't like how I got up with an 'attitude' so she decided to choke me to re establish her dominance in the home. When I removed her hand from my throat my little cousin came running out of his room like I was putting my hands on her. He instantly identified me as the abuser and began to protect his grandmother from the big, bad cousin.

He wrapped his arms around her as she began an Oscar worthy cry. She then said,

"I tried to help you I really did but you're done."

I told her that was fine and went to pack my things. Her and my little cousin then came and stood in the doorway blocking my exit. They stood watching me pack my things, like I was trash. They gave me some garbage bags to put my stuff in.

I told them that this was messed up how they were treating me. I had never done anything wrong to them. My little cousin said to Granny,

"Granny you don't have to say anything, Olivia it seems to me that your time here has expired."

At that point I had enough I said I needed to get something out of the bathroom I grabbed my things then when they moved to come back to watch me pack, I slammed the door and locked it before they could block me in again.

When I locked the door, I heard granny storm off. I then heard her husband say,

"O don't you go get that gun! Let her go"

I got my stuff and got out of there as fast as I could. Through the downpour of tears and hurt I prayed,

"Where to now Abba?"

I heard him say,

"Virginia."

# Chapter 49

## UNUSUAL RETURN

I made it to Virginia. I knew of some people there from when me and honey visited a few times. I contacted a few people I knew. One of the girls we used to hang out with, named Brandy, gave me some information concerning shelters, a good church, and she let me know if I ever wanted a plate to swing by. I appreciated her for that.

I contacted the shelter and they had some beds.

We did the intake, and I had a roof over my head. I sat on the bed and prayed,

> "Abba, what is my next assignment."

I waited for God to respond,

"Someone needs your guidance but be aware you are in the furnace, and it has been heated 7 times hotter."

I prepared myself for my assignment. I fasted and prayed

often.  I wanted to be sure that I slayed my flesh daily so that I could hear God clearly when He spoke to me. My self-appointed enemies became more strategic. I was aware, but I couldn't dwell.

After a week or so I walked into a diner for lunch.  The manager was walking in at the same time. I asked if they were hiring. She said yes and scheduled an interview for the next day. I got hired on the spot at my interview and started working the following day. I viewed this moment as confirmation that I am on the path God has for me.

I started to become more strategic with my prayers. I started asking God to reveal my enemies. I also asked God to give me the strength to handle the revelation. Next thing you know, people started to show their true colors around me. My work environment was becoming more toxic. I noticed that a lot of the new intakes at the shelter liked to hover around me vaguely paying attention to what I was doing. One woman literally sat at the door every day. It was almost like a veil had been lifted off my eyes and I could see.

I was careful not to get distracted by the revelations happening around me. I asked God to reveal my assignment. A couple hours later I met this young lady name "Grace". One day she was talking to a staff member while I was in the laundry room finishing up my laundry. I overheard her talking about some spiritual struggles she was having.

I couldn't help but interrupt,

"I'm sorry to get in yall conversation but that sounds like spiritual warfare you're going through. It sounds like you need deliverance. I know a thing or two about deliverance. I can help you if you want. Just let me know when you are ready."

She came to me a day later. I prayed with her and asked God what did He want me to say, and God said,
   "She must lay hands upon herself. You're not ready to lay hands. Tell her to lay hands on her head and to rebuke the demonic spirit, command the spirits to loose her, bind the spirits with chains of fire, and cast them to a dry baron land in the might name of Jesus. Have her read psalms 91 out loud. Tell her that above all she must believe she can be delivered."

We followed God's instructions. The next day she felt better. I heard God tell me,
                    "Job well done my child."
   It took a lot not to burst out in tears. I knew I was not worthy, but God saw something in me that I didn't see. I felt loved. I felt wanted.
   I quit my job at the diner when I was hired to be a caregiver at a group home for neurodivergent adults. I was so excited to be back in the field that I loved. When I started working in the home I was assigned too, the manager barely trained me. She would only offer guidance when I asked for it.
   She appeared to be nice in the interview but once I got into the house she switched up. I had experienced a few switch ups in my life, so I didn't allow this one to take my focus. I was just happy to be back in the field.
   A couple days later, I was sitting in my car at the shelter. I saw a moving truck pull in the parking lot. In the driver's seat of that truck was Maurice. We locked eyes and I went back to scrolling on my phone.
   The night before my move out date, I felt a stirring in my spirit. I prayed and asked God what was He trying to tell me. He replied,

"Don't go to sleep. Sit in the rec room by the door."

The shelter had a policy of collecting phones at night.  I stopped turning mine in at night. I did exactly what God told me to do. When the staff said I couldn't sit in the rec room I went to sit in the bathroom. When they needed to clean it I went to sit in the other bathroom. I made it through the night.

I praised God when I took my last shower there. I heard God say,

"They tried to kidnap you last night."

I praised Him again on my way out of the parking lot.

Later, I got a call from Brandy asking me if I wanted a plate. I said sure and thanked her for the offer. when I got there, I heard God say,

"Get out of there Now!"

There was great urgency in God's tone. I immediately obeyed. On my way out I saw five cars full of people with masks speed towards that location I was just at. I praised God with all my might. I knew my time was up here. I prayed and asked God where was He sending me. He said,

"Back to Oklahoma."

# Chapter 50

## GOD KEEPS HIS WORD

When I got back to Oklahoma City I pulled up to the hotel I stayed at last time, multiple cars pulled up. I immediately maneuvered my car so they couldn't block me in. I heard God say,

"Be still."

So, I sat and watched as they all went in the hotel. They all looked at me and laughed as they walked past my car.

"Stand your ground my child. I sent you here."

I gathered my things and went into the hotel. I waited for them to check in. while they were checking in the staff said she saw another room but it disappeared. I silently thanked God, For reminding me to make my reservation before I got there.

When they finished, I checked in and went to my room.

I praised God for His covering and settled in for the night. Before I went to bed I prayed for guidance.  He gave me a message,

"You are still surrounded my child. But I sent you here. Finish the book."

In the morning, I started back writing My book of poems. I got another job, but it didn't last long. Frustrated, I prayed to God for instructions.

"You have one week to finish this book…focus."

I did just that and I finished the book of poems. Everything started to move so fast. Three weeks later I submitted a query and got an agent. Within the next couple of months the book was ready for publishing. The following month I was signing a book deal with one of the best publishing companies in the country. Two weeks after my book hit the shelves. I went from being homeless to being a best-selling Author.  During each book event. I was able to hear how my poetry resonated with those who read it. I titled the collection,

"Grace to Beat the Odds"

My life did a complete turnaround.  I was no longer being stalked.  I had a home.  I was on T.V. doing interviews and interacting with powerful people. I had a home. I was traveling the world making lifelong connections. Did I mention that I had a home.

I became a motivational speaker. I knew this was God, I never even thought about motivational speaking. My collection of poems was nominated for many awards, including some of the most prestigious awards you can receive.

During this great move of God, I met a wonderful Man named David. He wasted no time asking me to be his wife. We had three amazing children. I was really living in abundance.

Chapter 50

As I laid out on the deck of our yacht. I thought about the promise God gave me in that jail cell. A promise of deliverance. I looked up at the sky as tears fell down my face.

*You really are a God of your word...Thank you Abba.*

# About the Author

For the past 2 years, Kendra Sterling has immersed herself into the world of writing.  She is originally from the Englewood neighborhood on the south side of Chicago. Life for her was far from perfect. Through the ups and downs, she stayed focused on her goal of becoming an Author.

Prior to her writing career, Kendra was a homeless, College drop-out. Refusing to let her setbacks define her, she began to write her debut fiction novel, 'Grace to Beat the Odds'.

When she is not writing you can find her watching her favorite movies and singing every musical number she knows as if she is standing on a Broadway stage and not in the shower.

www.ingramcontent.com/pod-product-compliance
Lightning Source LLC
Chambersburg PA
CBHW060320310726
48976CB00007B/2388